The Settlers' Journey

The Settlers'

Journey

Loch Ness to the
Murray River

SUSAN STOKES

ISBN: 978-0-6453263-0-7 (pbk)

eISNB: 978-0-6453263-1-4 (ebook)

A catalogue record for this
book is available from the
National Library of Australia

This book is dedicated to my family and friends.

Chapter One

On a chill August evening in the year 1851, Jane Sinclair stood beside the stove distractedly stirring simmering broth in a large cast iron pot. Its appetising aroma filled the cottage and very soon now the men would return, tired and hungry at the end of a long day. Summer and winter the fire burned. A large potage of vegetables was always stewing, while *tatties*, the staple diet of Scottish people, generally accompanied this. Methodically Jane removed a second pudding from the griddle and set it to one side; such was the requirement of four grown men! The Sinclairs' cottage was situated on the outskirts of Kirkfeldy, while their farm at the rear occupied a large area stretching to the base of Mt Drummock. James Sinclair's family had lived in the community for many generations, while Jane's mother's kin, the Cairns, were equally long residents of Glenkillen, a village some 16 miles to the north.

Running footsteps interrupted Jane's thoughts, as a breathless, eager and excited face appeared round the heavy wooden door. *'Janie, I won! I won the contest. Many of the boys couldn't do it, but I did. I lifted the hammer and threw it further than anyone else.*' The excitement and exuberance of yet another physical feat could not be contained. Jane's face lit up with joy at the shared triumph. Duncan, her youngest brother, whom she had raised from birth, was the light of her life. He was particularly thrilled to share this latest victory, just with her. Bored with Duncan, his older brothers generally found him a nuisance. Jane walked across to where he stood and hugged him. She embraced him as if she would never let go. Although just 8 years old, Duncan, like his father, was tall and robust; soon he would be a grown man. His affection for Jane was such that he did not protest, but when she finally released him, he looked at her with a puzzled expression. Never for a minute did he doubt her love and devotion to him, but as with people who care deeply for each other, a slight sense of unease stirred within him. The emotions and feelings aroused by that single gesture were disturbing. It was not out of character, but it was out of context, and the embrace said much more than well done, you know how proud of you I am. He studied her face searching for an indication of what it might mean, but nothing was forthcoming. Slowly he turned to the wooden frame where clothes were airing before the fire, and fulfilling his regular evening duty, folded them.

Shortly afterwards heavier footsteps were heard outside and the tiny kitchen area was filled to capacity. James Sinclair, an imposing man of six feet with a fine physique, sat down next to the fire and removed his boots. Although now stooped in his carriage, he was still a commanding figure. Beneath a grey beard and weather-beaten skin was the outline of a strong jaw, while perceptive eyes viewed the familiar scene. James greeted his daughter kindly and settled in his chair beside the fire while her brothers washed their hands and gathered round the table in anticipation of a hearty meal. Walter, Hunter and Gordon completed the Sinclair household.

Jane's mother had died in childbirth and since then, Jane, who was just 10 at the time, had cooked and kept house for her father and four brothers. She had taken the newborn baby under her wing and cared for him with such love and tenderness as scarce any child receives. Her father was a good and decent man, but a dour Scot with a puritanical streak. Indulgences and treats were not tolerated in the Sinclair household. But deep within, Jane knew that Duncan had been her saving grace, because she could spoil and indulge him. It wasn't just for Duncan, but also to fulfil a need in her, and thus she had been able to pour love, a fundamental part of her nature, into that special little boy.

James and his sons ate with great gusto, remaining at the table while Jane served second helpings. So much cooking was required just to meet their enormous appetites. Men who work outdoors always seem harder to satiate. The brothers talked among themselves and finally, when there was a temporary lull, Duncan enthusiastically relayed his feat. They nodded, but that was their only acknowledgement.

Jane, who had forced herself to eat, cleared the table and served the next course. Although it was late summer, a northerly wind blew and Gordon rose, pulling the casement shut. Jane tried to suppress the mounting tension inside her and concentrate on the task at hand. Now 18 years of age, she had never been under the illusion that life was easy. Jane loved and respected her father and her three grown-up brothers, who in turn cherished her, whilst her love for Duncan was special in a more protective way. Altogether different, however, were her feelings for Alistair MacLeay, an affection and attraction, which was the cause of her present dilemma. Jane loved him with all her heart and soul.

Alistair was Walter's age, and although he lived across the glen, he had been a constant and familiar sight at sports events and other gatherings. Their acquaintance had always been friendly and relaxed, until two years ago, when their feelings had taken on a new dimension. They fell in love and under normal circumstances, had this love been allowed to flourish, there would have been nothing extraordinary about it.

Lovers don't have to tell each other. It's in their eyes, it's in their hearts, it possesses their whole beings. Such was the love between Jane Sinclair and Alistair MacLeay. For a year, the pair had many occasions to share each other's company, but ever since Alistair had asked James Sinclair for his daughter's hand in marriage, the die had been cast. The thought of losing his live-in housekeeper ensured that the request was met with absolute refusal. Alistair was banned from seeing Jane and as a result both were utterly miserable. Initially, filial duty ensured Jane honoured her father's directive, but as time passed she became sadder. Duties and chores which she had happily fulfilled became a drudge to be resented, and last but not least she ached to see Alistair. A chance meeting assured her that he felt the same, but nothing further could be done. Thus it was that for almost six months they had lived in this frustrating situation.

In the eyes of James Sinclair, it was his daughter's duty to look after him and her brothers. That she had already done so admirably was of little consequence. Perhaps if she had been less diligent in her duties, it may have been easier for her to leave and lead a life of her own. Jane tried not to blame her father and instead just accepted that he was incapable of seeing her life and future from another viewpoint. However, Jane also knew that if she didn't leave with Alistair, she would never get away.

Some months after her father's refusal, Jane and Alistair had a brief encounter where a plan was devised and the lovers fled. Sadly, however, their exquisite happiness was short-lived. Enraged at having been defied and outwitted, James Sinclair despatched his two eldest sons on horseback to retrieve their errant sister. It was a humiliating experience for Jane, who was dragged back in a thoughtless and degrading manner. Forced to sit astride Walter's horse with Hunter riding beside them, Jane had no choice but to go with her forthright brothers, complying with their father's fierce directive. As the horses took off, Jane glanced back to see Alistair's heartbroken face. Their brief and magical time together, to say nothing of planned future happiness, had been dashed in an instant.

Alistair was devastated, but not defeated. Since resistance was futile, he had no choice but to stand back. Annoyed with himself for not having devised a better plan, he also acknowledged that he had not counted on the reaction of Jane's family. Thus it was that he returned to his farm dejected and suffering a mixture of emotions, mostly negative, but deep down there was still hope. This latest treatment of Jane by her father and brothers was to Alistair the last straw. She had always been so unselfish and dutiful in meeting their needs. He could not believe her brothers could treat her in this manner. It was as if she were not entitled to any say in her own life and certainly no happiness outside her immediate family. During the long journey home, not nearly as enjoyable as the one out, Alistair became adamant in his resolve to take Jane away. He knew deep down this was, most of all, for himself. In truth he could not imagine life without her, and so in some way he could see her family's viewpoint. But taking such a narrow and inflexible attitude would be very costly for the Sinclairs, and Alistair instinctively knew that Jane's love for him would overrule her devotion to her family. Yet it distressed him for her sake that their happiness had to be won at such a price. So when he finally reached Glen Morton, he did not return home but instead walked some distance to his brother's cottage. Not only did he feel the need to talk to someone, but he also wanted Archie's help and knew he could trust him implicitly.

Having failed once, Jane knew that tonight was their final attempt and she also understood that this time, Alistair would not fail. Her feelings were in so much tumult, because she knew this break with her family, who had been her life and her world to this date, would be irrevocable, and it was leaving Duncan that was breaking her heart. However, she dared tell no one of their plan, especially not her dear little brother, and that, of course, was the reason why she had earlier held and hugged him for so long. No opportunity had arisen for Jane to be apprised of exact plans, but this would be their final chance, with a destination, of necessity, far away. The heartbreak of leaving Duncan, still so vulnerable and dependent, was unbearable.

Earlier that afternoon Martha MacLeay, Archie's wife, had called hurriedly at the cottage with a brief message from Alistair. *'Take warm clothes. Archie has arranged for a boatman to ferry you across Loch Ness, from where you will travel to Dundee and catch a vessel to the Port of Leith. Upon arrival there, a resident clergyman, who has been contacted, will marry you.'* That was all Martha knew. Jane must not worry, but trust Alistair. With that she hugged Jane and gave her a tiny silver pendant, a family heirloom. It was all she could find that was valuable, sentimental and light enough to carry. What Jane did not know then, was that Archie and Martha had given Alistair a significant quantity of their savings, which, for them, was a sizeable amount. It was, of course, understood that the family farm then would belong entirely to Archie. Alistair saw this as a wonderful sacrifice on the part of his brother and sister-in-law, as ready money was essential to his plan and he had no other means of acquiring it. Even though the acquisition of the farm balanced out the deal, Alistair only ever saw the scheme in terms of a loan and was determined to repay his brother as soon as he was able.

The Highland Scots are a tough and formidable breed and Jane Sinclair was no exception. It wasn't a choice between good and bad, but it was a highly emotional decision with significant, long-term consequences. On the one hand, to leave her adored younger brother, who was still very dependent on her, and her father and three brothers. On the other, this was her only opportunity to join the man she loved, who was to be her life and future. Alistair offered Jane enduring love in a life of shared hope. The alternative was to continue in her present existence with no prospect of escape to a life of her own. Jane knew there would never be anyone else for her but Alistair, and so it was with this tumult of emotions that Jane Sinclair spent her last night with her family. As she truly divined, she would never see her father again.

Jane cleared away and washed the dishes. Seated beside the fire, James Sinclair drew down a book from the shelf, and read, as was his custom. They owned numerous books, which were treasured possessions and, unlike other farming folk in their district, Father read well. If not reading or reciting Robbie Burns, James Sinclair's favourite author was Walter Scott, so usually he read aloud from one of Scott's novels. The boys and Jane were encouraged to read also, but no one read as well as Father. Duncan was especially reluctant, and found reading difficult, but Jane and Father cajoled and encouraged him. When the chapter ended, Duncan said goodnight to his father and brothers, kissed Jane on the cheek and went up to bed. Jane did not trust herself to speak and was grateful that she had earlier experienced that all too brief opportunity to say goodbye.

The cottage was warm, cosy and secure. The boys stretched out in front of the hearth relaxing, as people who are physically exhausted do. Jane was not able to take in a visual picture of that all too familiar scene, because her eyes were filled with tears, so instead she closed them and listened to the stillness, broken only by the sounds of the burning log, the wind outside, and the puffing of her father's pipe. There hadn't been much for her to pack, because she had so few possessions, just her warmest clothing and a woollen rug from her bed.

Neither the boys nor their father noticed anything unusual as their sister mumbled goodnight and went up the little wooden staircase. She so badly wanted to visit Duncan, hug him, tell him she loved him and to ensure he understood that leaving him was breaking her heart. How could an 8-year-old understand? Yet Jane knew she could not risk telling him.

There would be no trousseau or honeymoon clothes for this bride, but that did not worry Jane. She knew her love for Alistair was true and that he, for her sake, also was leaving family, friends and everything that was familiar and precious to him. Martha had not said where they would ultimately be going. It was an unknown destination, with neither family and friends nor financial security to fall back on, but the alternative she did know, and although it was certain, it offered no intimate love such as she would share with Alistair, nor any hope of change. Earlier in the day Jane had packed just a few possessions in her tapestry bag. Because everything, as well as food, had to be carried, and conscious of the Highlands over which they would be trekking, weight was a significant factor, therefore only essentials were stowed in her bag. Jane's outdoor boots by the front door would be her only shoes, just one night-dress, two skirts and two blouses, a woollen shawl, rug and last but not least, a warm woollen coat.

Accepting now that nothing further could be done, Jane dressed herself for their journey, then lay down on her bed and quietly waited until her father and brothers also retired. A brief note lay on her dressing table, advising of her departure with Alistair. Although Jane felt unbelievable tension, she knew that all her strength would be needed for the forthcoming journey. Martha's pendant round her neck felt like a special talisman. In the larder was a small basket of provisions Jane had prepared to sustain them until they could safely obtain food.

The wait seemed interminable, but eventually Jane heard the scraping of chairs and general motion as the group downstairs prepared to retire. She refused to allow herself any more distress in relation to Duncan, and promised herself that as soon as she felt secure and safe, wherever that might be, she would write to her father, begging his forgiveness and advise him of her condition and location. She then would confide her distress at leaving. Jane knew instinctively that Alistair would look after her, care for her, and protect her, but that she, too, would need to be strong in this endeavour, and that meant not allowing herself to feel more anxiety or distress than she could help. It was clear this would not be an adventure for someone faint-hearted, and that her health, not only in the form of food and rest, but in emotional stability also, was essential.

When eventually the household fell silent, Jane made a decision to risk going sooner rather than later. The fear of her brothers coming after them again was real. That she and Alistair must put as much distance as possible between them before daylight, when her disappearance would be discovered, was essential. Silently she slipped downstairs, collected her basket from the larder, and took a quick final glance at her home of 18 years, before putting on her boots, opening the front door and stepping out.

Alistair dared not come too near the cottage, so Jane walked some distance along the pathway before she saw him. Waiting under a tree, he hurried out to greet her. Because their relationship had been so suppressed, the sight and feel of each other was overwhelming. They clung tightly in a long embrace. No words were spoken; just being together was heaven, as they experienced that special sensation which only lovers know – a temporary trance of relief and joy. The reality of their situation, however, soon intruded, and they hastened onwards. Jane gave just one anxious glance behind. The memory of their last elopement was indelibly printed on both their minds. They understood only too well that their long-term happiness depended on getting as far away from Kirkfeldy as swiftly as they could.

Chapter Two

ALISTAIR'S BELONGINGS AND SUCH EQUIPMENT AS THEY would need were strapped to his back and, in addition, he carried a woven bag which Martha had stitched for him. On such a long and treacherous journey, weight and convenience were significant factors. Once they were down the hill and out of sight of the cottage, Alistair followed the road for about two and a half miles before leaving the pathway and taking a course across the mountains. It was strenuous walking up a steep incline densely covered with heather, but fortunately providence favoured them with a cloudless night and a bright moon. *'It will be difficult terrain, and much slower, but this way we're less likely to be followed,'* was Alistair's justification. *'But where are we going?'* Jane asked in some surprise. *'The Port of Leith,'* and in answer to her puzzled expression, he confounded her even further, by adding, *'And then, to New South Wales.'* Her only answer was a gasp, followed by a look of horror. Jane, however, recovered quickly, made no further comment and strode ahead. Many years later Alistair would often recall her simple response and trusting reaction, reinforcing his lifelong endearment of her. It was a mixture of love, faith and courage. Jane's knowledge of settlement in New South Wales pertained mostly to convicts.

The night was mild except for a northerly wind, so that it was comfortable when sheltered in the glen, but bracing on the hills. Fortunately, the moon was bright and the surrounding scenery spectacular, but regrettably there was no time to look up and admire it. Watching where one stepped across this rugged terrain was what mattered. They didn't speak much, walking on as swiftly as they could, hoping this time there would be no sound of horsemen on their trail.

After trudging for about three hours they took a short rest, sitting on some ancient stones, while they ate Jane's provisions. Alistair produced a simple gold band from his pocket and slipped it on her finger. *'It is a bit soon, my darling, but I want you to wear it,'* he said. Simple as the gesture was, it spoke more than words. A long and tender embrace followed before they set off again, still mindful of their goal – to get as far away as they could before daybreak. Gifts were a rarity for Jane, so to receive two in one day was a new experience. She felt a warm inner glow, created by the awareness of the band on her finger, the locket round her neck and Alistair by her side. Instead of facing an arduous trek, which in other circumstances would have been fearful and exhausting, their after-dark Highland escapade seemed almost a joy. Much as they had to share, few words were spoken. The most important thing was to focus on the ground before their feet. The heather was dense and there were dangerous divots and holes. *'Would it be easier to hold my hand?'* Alistair asked, but Jane thought it safer, especially over the densely covered mountains, to follow in his footsteps. All she hoped was that her departure would not be discovered before daybreak.

Rested and refreshed after a brief stop, they walked for another two hours before reaching the summit of the furthest mountain. The Loch below looked spectacular. Like a wide silver ribbon, which buckled and folded in a careless, untidy manner, the water stretched out in the moonlight, spreading to low-lying areas. This was further than Jane had ever been in her life and she paused for a moment, breathless, enjoying the beautiful view. Her knowledge of New World colonies was negligible, but she was certain that such beautiful scenery would not be seen there. They descended down to the water's edge where Alistair found his instructions to be accurate. A rough path followed the loch in a southerly direction, and although it took them another hour of trekking, it was less strenuous than the earlier terrain they had crossed. Just as dawn was breaking, they caught sight of a small village.

A high path along the hill provided a backdrop to the settlement, thereby skirting the village. The wind dropped and everything was still and silent as they looked down on cottages huddled together on either side of a narrow, cobbled street. A farmyard dog barked as they passed, but otherwise all was silent. Some distance beyond the village,

Alistair recognised a small hamlet which had been described to him; however, he believed it was too early to call. A copse of trees directly above the cottage provided welcome shelter where they settled down to rest and enjoy the remainder of their provisions. Some half hour later, candlelight appeared in the window of the cottage, so they set off again.

In response to Alistair's knock, a man with a ruddy complexion, dressed in woollen stockings and breeches, opened the door and quietly listened to their story, before ushering them inside. He explained that within the hour he would cross Loch Ness, before travelling to a village to bring back supplies. The boatman's wife came into the kitchen with a toddler on her hip, whom she placed in a simple harness with some bread while she bustled to meet their needs. Jane was offered a bowl of warm water to wash herself, before they were served steaming porridge. The boatman's provender was already packed and waiting by the door, but his kindly wife busied herself and in no time had arranged a generous supply of food, as much as she could spare, for Jane and Alistair's next journey.

Thanking her for much kindness, they put on their boots and set off with her burly husband. For so large and cumbersome a man, he launched the boat and handled the oars with great dexterity. The water was as smooth as glass, and the couple watched, fascinated, as the oarsman, with easy strokes, propelled his craft across the loch. Farther than it appeared, they reached the other side some three-quarters of an hour later.

After securing his small craft, they set off on foot with the boatman to the village of Spey, where he was evidently well known, since he was greeted with friendly smiles. The name of a man with a cart, who for a fee could take them a considerable distance towards the coast, was given to Alistair.

Mindful of Jane's family who by now would be on their trail, Alistair paid the carrier, and after seating was found for them on the densely loaded cart, they sallied forth. It wasn't the most comfortable journey, but far greater distance was covered than the pair could ever have managed on foot.

Apart from feeling relief as their cart set off, Jane now realised she could actually look at the countryside, instead of keeping her eyes on the ground, a necessity during their strenuous trek over dense heather and steep, rough terrain. Nestling beside Alistair who had his arm around her, Jane gazed at the beautiful green hills, darker mountains beyond, and wonderful foliage. The Sinclair brothers had made some excursions, but Jane had never ventured beyond the Kirkfeldy district. As their cart rattled along the track before turning round a high stone-covered escarpment, one of the most spectacular sights of their journey was suddenly revealed. A smooth mirror-like loch spread for miles. Across this firth, in the distance, masses of water surged over high rocks, plunging into the inlet below.

Observing Jane's reaction, Alistair called Iain, their

carrier, to please pause temporarily, so they could take in this magnificent view. In light of their circumstances, it was only a momentary stop, but this beautiful vision would always be remembered. Alistair had not travelled far either, but he did share with Jane a memorable trip he and Archie had made when quite young. In the depth of winter at their father's request, the lads had ridden to Inverness. It was a challenging trip, but unquestionably the most memorable feature was the entire snow-covered landscape. Everything had been white as far as the eye could see. *'Imagine if we had tried to elope in winter? It would have been impossible,'* Alistair mused. Quietly Jane replied, *'Well, even now in summer, trekking across the Highlands is bitterly cold. I am so glad I packed my warmest clothes. To reach the coast with you, and feel safe from my father, is really all that I wish.'* A long embrace followed. Hopefully they would soon be free, and uncertain though their future was, how wonderful it felt, just to be together, while sharing this precarious expedition to the southern hemisphere!

After another day of bumpy riding and modest overnight shelter, Alistair and Jane eventually reached a village, the closest point eastwards to which the carrier would travel. With a final farewell, they shook hands, thanked Iain and found a quiet stream, where they washed and indulged themselves with a well-earned rest before eating the last rations provided by the boatman's wife. Thankfully, so far they had been safe, but by now horsemen in the form of

Jane's brothers would definitely be on their trail. The warmth of Alistair's arm around her and his loving affection were things Jane couldn't wait to experience more of, eventually, in an environment free of tension. All had worked well to date, but they were still vulnerable. The east coast was just several hours' walking distance, the driver had told them. Much as Jane wished to lie down and rest with her adored Alistair in this beautiful scenic valley, they gathered their few possessions and set off for what they hoped would be their final trek.

Two hours of steady walking occupied them until early in the afternoon, they reached the crest of a hill and viewed beneath them the spectacular Scottish coastline with green hills sloping down to the sea. In the distance, alongside the Firth of Tay, was Dundee. What a relief it was to be here! Tall masts of several sailing ships in the estuary, as well as church spires, formed a distinctive backdrop. Outbuildings and warehouses lined the firth, while a wharf extended from the waterfront. Since Jane had never seen the sea, several moments of fascination and reflection were spent just admiring the view.

To have reached the coast brought a huge sense of both relief and accomplishment; however, much more was still to be achieved, so despite their fatigue, the pair continued, walking through the town to the dock, where Alistair enquired about a passage to the Port of Leith. It took some time, but eventually they were directed to an English sea captain, who, to their delight and amazement, announced he was heading south shortly. For what seemed a princely sum, he agreed to take them. Alistair paid, and assisted by the captain, the lovers climbed aboard. Exhausted, Jane sat down on the deck, finally feeling a sense of freedom and relief at not needing to look over her shoulder. Pursuit of them now would be no mean feat.

The North Sea, normally wild and formidable, was calm and gentle on that late summer afternoon. As the ship swayed leisurely with the motion of the waves, the weary pair relaxed and waited for the sails to be unfurled and the anchor drawn up. Fortunately, the weather remained calm, so their first seafaring voyage was both fascinating and comfortable. As it was just a short distance, the ship sailed within sight of the coast, enabling them to observe Scotland's beautiful rugged coastline.

The Port of Leith was overflowing with ships so that significant time was required before the vessel could anchor, by which time darkness had set in. Numerous passengers were scheduled to board the vessel in the morning for a voyage to London and then across the Atlantic. Observing his young passengers, clearly unfamiliar with their location, the captain very kindly agreed to accommodate Jane and Alistair overnight. Extremely grateful, they thanked him heartily. At sunrise, they made their farewells and went ashore in search of Reverend Samuel Cobden to whom Archie had written and sent birth records from their parish.

Chapter Three

AFTER LEAVING THE DOCK AREA, THEY CAME UPON AN exclusive neighbourhood with the grandest houses Jane had ever seen. Ladies and gentlemen in the streets were very finely attired. Jane's wardrobe, in contrast, comprised simple dresses sewn by herself, to say nothing of her Highland boots.

Coming upon a lovely stone church with old graves in the surrounding area, they admired the beautiful garden around the rectory before deciding to inquire for Reverend Cobden. Answering the door, a young maid greeted them with a bright smile but said they would need to cross the bridge over the Water of Leith in order to find the minister in question. Then, once in that district, she was sure anyone would be able to direct them to his manse.

As two young people who had never left the Highlands, they were suddenly overwhelmed with new sights, smells and experiences. Jane found the speech and different accents intriguing. She had always imagined that everyone who spoke English communicated as they did, yet now within a few days she had heard numerous dialects, including a deckhand whom she could barely understand, even though his native tongue was English. Activities around them, as well as the totally different and stimulating environment, diminished their weariness.

The other side of the river revealed a completely diverse settlement, and certainly a different society. As they turned into a narrow street, both felt overwhelmed by the poverty. Houses were small, little more than hovels, with no gardens. In place of cobbled streets, dusty lanes provided access, which doubtless would be muddy quagmires in winter. A group of children playing in the street eyed them curiously. Alistair asked where they might find Reverend Cobden, and immediately they responded with excitement, running ahead to direct the visitors. Most of the youngsters were barefoot, with dirty faces and threadbare clothes. The surroundings did not improve and Alistair began to wonder about Archie's recommendation, when suddenly the children disappeared through a gate, and they found themselves standing in a gravelled courtyard, where one of the boys pulled the bell at a rear door. The rectory was behind the church and it seemed the children had brought them to the back entrance. Neither Jane nor Alistair had seen the small house of worship.

A middle-aged, well-dressed lady, with kindly eyes and a smiling face, opened the door. She spoke softly to the children, calling many by name and quietly listened to their excited voices as they introduced the visitors. Thanking the familiar youngsters, she ushered the young couple inside. They walked through the kitchen to a cosy sitting room where sun shone through south-facing casements. It was only small, but everything was in perfect taste, with ornaments and lovely paintings. Mrs Cobden rang for tea, then listened to their tale. Jane observed the beautiful tea service, exquisite cloth and hands unused to manual labour. This lady seemed incongruous in the poverty-stricken neighbourhood. Yes, Mrs Cobden said, her husband was expecting them. Normally several days would be required before a wedding ceremony could be performed, but since her husband had all their papers, she was sure it could be speedily arranged. Presently he was comforting a bereaved family, but he would be home shortly.

After listening to their story, Mrs Cobden insisted they stay at the rectory until a ship sailed. She had two married daughters in the south of England, and although she loved their visits, the girls journeyed north rarely. Jane was ensconced in the guest room, while a bed was arranged for Alistair in a little chamber at the rear.

Samuel Cobden duly arrived and proved to be a delightful man. His face had rather an aesthetic look, but when he smiled, his whole appearance changed revealing pleasing, expressive eyes. No wonder his parishioners loved him. All hours of the day or night, in all weathers, Samuel Cobden was available to minister to their needs. Albeit only a brief acquaintanceship, and despite many years' difference in age, the MacLeays' and Cobdens' complementary friendship was one which was to survive vast distances and a lifetime. The MacLeays managed to assist several emigrant families, sponsored by Reverend Cobden, to settle in the colony of New South Wales.

The following afternoon, in her Sunday dress, Jane Sinclair married Alistair MacLeay. There were no guests, just Samuel Cobden, who performed the ceremony, with his wife Elizabeth as witness. Vastly different as it was to most weddings, the minister and his wife doubted neither the sincerity of the vows, nor the depth of their love. Great sacrifices had been made by this young couple, but love would sustain them, as they faced a long, treacherous voyage to an unknown future in a foreign land.

Their honeymoon consisted of a walk through the local neighbourhood, dinner with the Cobdens and finally sharing themselves in the small guest bedroom that night. To Alistair nothing could have been more perfect. Gratitude to this kind minister and his wife was profound. Their own resources did not stretch to good accommodation, yet they could not have wished for a more perfect ending to their special day.

Early the following morning, Alistair woke with the most exquisite feeling of joy and happiness. After the strain of the last few months and the torture of being separated from his adored Jane, he could scarcely believe the present was real. Resting on one elbow, he watched as she breathed peacefully beside him. The exhaustion of the past week had ensured a profound sleep. Her slightly parted lips revealed even teeth, while her beautiful profile was relaxed and serene. Strands of fair hair, usually tied back, lay loose and free about her face, revealing flawless skin so soft to touch. Alistair felt a deep sense of gratitude that this beautiful girl, whom he had adored for so long, was finally his. He wasn't an idealist. Their future was an unknown risk, but deep within, a sense of peace prevailed that with Jane, regardless of pain and sacrifice, they would somehow survive. As he lay down again, she opened her eyes and smiled as he drew her to him.

Alistair believed it might take some time to secure a passage to the colonies of the southern hemisphere, but here Reverend Cobden once again came to their rescue. His friend from a neighbouring district, Reverend George Kerr, was taking a group of young impoverished lads to the newly settled Port Phillip District. Unlike Sydney and Hobart Town, Port Phillip was not a convict settlement. A recently returned sea captain had relayed that extensive building was occurring there, both public and private. Tradesmen were required, and, as in their homeland, Mechanics Institutes had been established in all three settlements, Sydney, Hobart Town and the Port Phillip District, recently named Melbourne. Membership at a Mechanics Institute would assist these lads, whose education was limited. Reverend Kerr also hoped that a warmer climate might ameliorate the poor health of several boys. A generous benefactor, the Laird of Glencairn, had contributed money towards their migration, and Reverend Kerr was hopeful that some funds might be available to ensure their membership of a Mechanics Institute in the colony, where necessary skills could be improved and acquired.

By reason of the above, Jane and Alistair realised they may only have a day or two before departure, and thus hastened to the rectory kitchen for breakfast. Hopefully Reverend Cobden's recommendation would ensure their inclusion aboard this vessel bound for New South Wales, but it was not certain. They therefore walked to the dock hoping to meet the captain and view his ship.

It was a glorious summer day. Trees were in full leaf and brightly coloured flowers bloomed in gardens and parks. The sun felt warm and invigorating as they strolled arm in arm. The Port was still occupied with numerous vessels, but after several enquiries they were directed to Samuel Cobden's contact.

Anchored at the quay, the *Esperance* was 400 tons and just over 100 feet long. It had been overhauled, and was setting sail for New South Wales the following day. As it was virtually a full ship, with some 190 passengers and 26 crew, Jane and Alistair were lucky to have Reverend Cobden's influence, ensuring they could be accommodated. Jane thought the *Esperance* looked particularly small for so long and treacherous a voyage, but she was reassured on two points: one, that after extensive repairs and maintenance, the ship was sound, and secondly, that the *Esperance* had made this same journey several times. The latter, in fact, was the more heartening. Captain Edmondson was an experienced seaman, equipped with a lifetime of sailing. He greeted them warmly, while the MacLeays, with a mixture of relief and apprehension, joined other emigrants sailing to the southern hemisphere.

A young man, who was also giving the ship critical appraisal, introduced himself to Alistair as Ewan Mortimer from Yorkshire. As they shook hands, this friendly fellow said that he too was sailing on the *Esperance*. His enthusiasm was infectious and certainly helped Jane feel less apprehensive about their forthcoming voyage. At the direction of his father, a wealthy merchant, Ewan had accepted a position with his uncle, Hugh Mortimer, at the Port Phillip District, to manage a large run alongside a northern river. Ewan did not intend to remain in the colony forever, but he was looking forward to this expedition and hoped, with assistance, to produce large quantities of wool on his uncle's sheep station for shipment to his father's Yorkshire mill. A school friend of Ewan's in the Royal Navy, who had visited New South Wales, had inspired his friend with tales of wonder and excitement at what was being achieved there. It was accepted that eventually Ewan would inherit his father's woollen mill. The breeding of sheep and production of wool on a vast scale, namely, sourcing the actual raw material, was felt to be an invaluable factor in the ongoing success of the mill, especially in the eyes of his father. Mindful that it might be years before he returned to his homeland, Ewan had travelled north to visit his sister and her family at Leith, departing from there, rather than travelling south to London.

After lengthy discourse with this fellow traveller, Alistair and Jane finalised arrangements and payment of their passage with Captain Edmondson, before returning to the hospitable Cobdens. So much had happened in the last few days that Jane's life at Kirkfeldy already seemed a world away. She thought many times of Duncan, but only spoke of him once to Alistair. There was nothing she could do about it and mixed with those feelings for her dearly loved brother was the dreadful retribution which would be exacted if she ever returned. So there was nothing else but to store in her heart those treasured memories and set the remainder free. Jane did not wish to harbour dark recollections of the past and, indeed, there were so many new experiences to savour daily instead. All the money in the world could not buy her handsome, courageous and humorous Alistair. She adored him.

Other than a troupe of gypsies and one or two pedlars on the road between Spey and Dundee, they had met with good fortune and encountered delightful people. Jane was not so naïve as to think that this always would be so, but decided nevertheless to enjoy life while it was trouble free and certainly now, with Alistair, each day was one to be treasured.

Jane's apprehension regarding their ultimate destination was significantly increased when Reverend Cobden presented

Alistair with a tent, which had been donated to the parish. The Minister relayed that from stories he had heard it could well be a valuable asset upon landing either at Botany Bay or the Port Phillip District, in the event accommodation was not readily available. Mindful of his limited funds, Alistair thanked Samuel with heartfelt gratitude.

During their last few days in Scotland, Elizabeth Cobden, who had observed Jane's meagre possessions, presented her with two dresses she no longer required. Usually, old clothes were given to parishioners, but these she had chosen especially for her house guest, and clearly, with much thought. One dress was of a dark, heavy serge material suitable for cold weather. Accompanying it was a warm woollen vest and thick shawl. The second frock was of a light cotton fabric, suitable for hot summer days. Stout boots and a wide-brimmed bonnet were also included. Jane was extremely touched, especially as her own needs had barely been considered during her life's recent upheaval. Under the circumstances, these gifts were of immeasurable value and Elizabeth Cobden's gesture was never forgotten.

As requested by Captain Edmondson, the next morning Jane and Alistair carried their possessions on board and packed them into a tiny cabin, accessed down a steep flight of steps at the rear of the ship, adjacent to the crew. It was extremely confined, but at least they had some privacy and were not sharing bunks in the open area with the emigrant passengers. Without Reverend Cobden's intervention this accommodation never would have been offered. Observing that their cubicle was some distance from the privy – a bucket set down a hole inside a small closet – Alistair accepted a wooden pail from Captain Edmondson for their own exclusive use. At night and during storms privy access could become hazardous. Daily, Alistair was able to lower their bucket on a rope into the sea, rinsing it, and they were spared long delays in the emigrant queue. Ewan Mortimer's accommodation on the upper deck was completely different. Like other first class passengers, he had a more spacious cabin, and only a select few had access to their private and more spacious water closet, which was emptied and cleaned by crew members daily. While waiting for the anchor to be drawn up and for the ship to set sail, Alistair and Jane watched as sheep, pigs, cows, ducks and chickens were taken on board for the journey.

Chapter Four

WHEN THEY HAD BEEN AT SEA ONLY ONE WEEK AND HAD not as yet experienced bad weather, Jane acknowledged to herself that she would never see Scotland again. Whatever thoughts she had had in relation to this prior to setting sail, she knew she could not endure another sea voyage. Regardless of the perils that lay ahead in their new homeland, she believed they would be easier than a journey by sea. She didn't say much to Alistair, because so many people on board probably felt as she did and it was best to talk of other subjects: either families and loved ones at home, or what they hoped to achieve in the new colony. Alistair found it exhilarating to watch the skills of sailors, as they quickly and effortlessly climbed rope ladders and unfurled sails, and then, as a consequence, to feel the vessel gather or slacken speed. The ship was everything to these young lads, who gave their all when called upon, even if it meant risking their lives. Alistair thrilled watching their unquestioning call to duty, regardless of the time or the request. It entailed their own safety, as well as the passengers', but clearly respect for their captain was unquestioned.

Deep down Jane felt that Alistair would love to be part of it all, rather than an idle spectator. The athleticism of these young men, scrambling up rope ladders at breakneck speed, before expertly balancing on ropes as sails were unfurled, was extraordinary. What would it be like in a storm once they reached the roaring forties? But there was no sense in thinking that far ahead, Jane tried to remind herself. They were fine now and safely afloat. That neither she, nor Alistair suffered from seasickness, like many of the other passengers, was something for which she was exceptionally grateful. Observing horrendous and compulsive vomiting among passengers was hideous. Fear of drowning was real, but to worry about it was pointless. All one could do was trust in Captain Edmondson and his dutiful and talented crew.

Accompanying their friend Ewan to his cabin on the upper deck, Jane observed muskets lined up near the Captain's Table, which she found somewhat unnerving. Britain was not at war. Why would guns be in such a prominent and accessible location? Captain Edmondson relayed that they had never been required during his sailing experience, but they were, nevertheless, essential. Shocking incidents had occurred, where becalmed ships near the equator had been attacked by pirates. After stealing all valuable cargo, the crew and passengers sometimes had been murdered. The ships then were either abandoned or ruthlessly sunk. Guns were also essential to maintaining order in the event of unruly or mutinous passengers below decks. As a young sailor, Captain Edmondson had observed his skipper use muskets to bring a recalcitrant thug under control. In the interests of everyone aboard, it had been necessary to place the ruffian in irons until he could be offloaded. Jane discussed this story only with Alistair; it was very frightening.

Daily, Alistair spent hours observing, with a mixture of fascination and envy, the clockwork operation of Captain Edmondson's ship and recording their latitude and longitude, so as to gauge the distance travelled. Jane, however, felt less than comfortable. For her, it was impossible to remain impervious to the sudden lurches and crashes as the vessel plunged into deep troughs. The timber creaked and groaned as if it would come asunder. At night this was particularly unnerving. Having been used to fresh Highland air, sleeping was especially unpleasant, with putrid odours, and wails from people below, either sick or crying out in panic. The basis of Jane's discomfort was fear. She was terrified of drowning, and living with this constant dread was a hideous trial. She endeavoured to pacify her nerves with the thought that the captain and crew had undertaken this same voyage many times, in fact had chosen this as a way of life. She worked hard to stay calm, as she knew that poor diet and other privations inseparable from months at sea would inevitably take their toll on the health of many passengers.

One very positive distraction, however, was the teacher

whom Reverend Kerr had brought to accompany his young tradesmen. Daily, regardless of weather or other upheavals, Mr Anderson gathered his young men and instructed them in Mathematics and English. As each class ended, an exercise was set which was to be completed before the next day's session. It was both invaluable instruction and a perfect occupation for idle young men on a long, treacherous and at times boring voyage.

Mealtimes left a lot to be desired. Porridge at breakfast, boiled meat and vegetables at midday, followed by broth at teatime. A bell was rung a certain number of times to indicate which meal it was. It wasn't so much the substance of the food, which was adequate, albeit always the same, but the method of serving and eating that Jane objected to. Some people pushed and shoved to get served first, while manners among others were non-existent, which was not conducive to a good appetite. Low benches beside tables ran the length of the main dining area on the lower deck, which also doubled as the entertainment area for everyone to pass the time when the weather was inclement. Sometimes a stale odour remained. So far the elements had been kind, despite being windswept on deck. After Ewan Mortimer approached the captain, and when the weather was calm, Alistair and Jane were invited to dine at the Captain's Table, served on the forecastle. This provided a most refreshing change, which Jane valued. Just eating with people in a civilised manner was pleasing.

They passed several brigs. Two of them hoisted the Tricolour, and acknowledgement of the French was respectful. Eventually they approached a vessel flying the British ensign, and as the ships edged closer, *The Searcher* could be read emblazoned on its bow. Horns were sounded before a boat was lowered and basic goods were transferred. Two months out of Sydney with a cargo of wool, *The Searcher*'s captain sent across oranges, raisins, and of particular interest, some Sydney newspapers. After the captain and upper deck passengers had perused them, they were passed on to Alistair.

At Tenerife the *Esperance* anchored and extra provisions were taken aboard. Jane would love to have set foot on solid ground, but just crew members and several upper deck male passengers were allowed ashore. At least, however, a reasonable part of the trip was behind them. Alistair loved birds and watched for hours their effortless flight behind the schooner as they dived into the wake, circling back and forth. Porpoises, too, joined in the chase, leaping high in the air, diving deep and coming up beside or ahead of the vessel.

Once, they saw a school of whales and Alistair marvelled at the enormous size of these prehistoric creatures, the length of the *Esperance*, fanning their tails, and raising their enormous bulk out of the water, while spouting spray some 20 feet in the air. These magnificent ocean beasts proved to be another source of fear to Jane. Despite her best efforts to sleep after that, she constantly woke with each ache and groan of the ship, sure it was a whale, tossing them aloft in one casual motion. The first mate, Malcolm, was a former whale man who had spent several years in the south seas aboard an American whaler. A giant of a man, Malcolm was extremely strong and an expert seaman. He watched the mammals with enormous frustration, muttering and complaining that *'out there was pounds of oil, which couldn't be accessed'*. The rest of the crew treated him with a reasonable amount of caution. Although a skilled sailor, he had a fiery temper and an unpredictable disposition. His entire life had been spent at sea and he had no family.

Eventually, with a mixture of relief and nervous excitement, after weeks of nothing but the monotony of the ocean, they finally sighted the African coast. The *Esperance* sailed parallel to the shoreline before entering Cape Town Harbour. Winds straight from the South Pole tore at them as they braced themselves on deck. Despite the freezing conditions, many people came up to enjoy views of their only real port of call. Table Mountain framed behind the township looked spectacular. The ship remained in the harbour for several days, while vegetables, fruit and livestock were taken on board. The MacLeays loved this respite. Thanks to Ewan Mortimer's influence, they were included with a small group permitted to go ashore. Walking round the township, they absorbed the foreign sights, smells, vegetation and buildings. Once again Alistair was intrigued at the variety of strange birds, which he had, of course, never seen before. Fruit and vegetables unobtainable in Scotland were sampled, and Jane again found she was drawn to people's speech. Another novelty was seeing friendly local people and especially their beautiful children. The atmosphere in Cape Town was one of contentment. It seemed different to Scotland and Jane wondered whether a milder climate might be a factor. She would have been happy to disembark here and make this their home. It was not so far from Scotland, and would have spared them the next treacherous stage of their voyage.

Eventually the *Esperance*, fortified and hastily refurbished, set sail. Much to Jane's discomfort they headed due south. According to Captain Edmondson, the further south they sailed, the quicker their passage. Jane was not sure, however, which was the worse of two evils: a longer voyage, or more treacherous seas. Now they were well and truly in the southern hemisphere, and Alistair studied the stars with fascination.

However, it was not the sea that was to cause their next sorrow. Just a week after they departed Cape Town, Ewan Mortimer became seriously ill. There was no prior warning; he simply woke in the night with excruciating abdominal pain. An attractive man whom they both had grown to love, Ewan was wonderful company, entertaining and amusing. He had a unique sense of humour, was a gifted raconteur and had added a special dimension to their journey. His infectious enthusiasm spread to everyone. He was first and foremost an Englishman, proud of his country and conscious of his duty to portray himself as such. So hearing him cry out in agonised pain was a sign he was seriously ill. No doctor was on board, and even if there had been, it's doubtful that anything could have been done. Suffering from acute appendicitis, Ewan Mortimer endured another 24 hours of torment before dying of blood poisoning from a burst appendix. Despite his feeling of helplessness, Alistair scarcely left Ewan's side during that time. Captain Edmondson issued rum to alleviate the worst of his agony. During a few spells of relief when he lay exhausted, the dying man handed Alistair some papers and requested they be taken to his uncle, Hugh Mortimer, when they arrived at the Port Phillip settlement. Alistair promised he would do anything he was asked, but hoped and prayed that would not be necessary.

In addition to Ewan's excruciating pain, it was clear there was another underlying burden of which he needed to be relieved. After listening to weak entreaties and following a pointing finger, Alistair delved into Ewan's trunk only to discover it had a false bottom. Eventually, after penetrating the base with a knife, it split open, revealing a sizeable sum of money. In a weak, breathless whisper, Ewan managed to reveal that he was transporting pound notes, at his father's request, to his uncle. In Henry Mortimer's view, the breeding of sheep with its ensuing production of wool, on a vast scale, would be an invaluable factor in the ongoing success of his Yorkshire mill. To that end, and as an incentive to his brother in the colony, Henry Mortimer had contributed a substantial sum to this New South Wales venture. Unsure whether an English cheque would be recognised in the colony, Ewan's father had provided money.

Alistair had no qualms about delivering papers, but he certainly could have done without this considerable responsibility. Already carefully guarding the remaining pounds Archie had given him, neither he nor Jane needed this burden, but what could they do? Of course, he reassured his dying friend that upon his life, the exact sum would be handed to his uncle. Appreciating that Alistair's integrity was beyond question, it was with an enormous sense of relief that Ewan closed his eyes. Another hour of suffering was to be endured before he died. Devastated that his support and entreaties for Ewan were in vain, Alistair, after first ensuring the pound notes were safely concealed, lay down on his bunk, physically and emotionally exhausted.

The following day, Ewan's body was sewed into a hammock with several weights, to ensure that it sank when committed to the deep. It was placed on the quarterdeck where the passengers were seated. The British flag was lowered to half-mast and the ship laid to, while Reverend Kerr read the burial service before releasing Ewan's body into the ocean. It was a very distressing ceremony. The Minister had performed two equally tragic burials for a baby and a small child, but their close friendship with Ewan exacerbated the MacLeays' grief; this day would never be forgotten.

Alistair and Jane felt a great sense of loss. Ewan's

enthusiasm and eagerness to reach the colony had served to alleviate some of their anxiety and foreboding. His death was deeply mourned. Alistair wrote a detailed letter to Ewan's parents in Yorkshire, describing exactly the circumstances of their son's death and expressing to them his and Jane's profound grief and Ewan's impact on his fellow travellers during the voyage. He reassured them that in line with their son's wishes, everything would be carefully and honourably conveyed to Hugh Mortimer upon their arrival in the colony. Captain Edmondson agreed that Alistair should take responsibility for all Ewan's personal effects and arrange delivery of them. In turn, Captain Edmondson undertook to ensure safe conveyance of Alistair's letter to the Mortimer family in England.

At this time, Jane realised that Captain Edmondson also would be the most reliable person to convey a message to her own family. She therefore composed the following letter, which was left in the captain's safekeeping, to dispatch on his return to England.

Dear Father,

Alistair MacLeay and I were married at Port of Leith on 20th August, by Reverend Samuel Cobden. We are on our way to New South Wales and plan to disembark at the Port Phillip District. We are well and I am sorry to have caused you distress. Captain Edmondson has agreed to forward this letter to you upon his return,

*so that you will not be wondering about me. As and
when we are settled, I shall write again. I miss you all
very much, especially Duncan. The journey has been
hazardous, but we are nearing our destination.
I remain as always your loving daughter,
Jane*

Letters to the Cobdens and Archie and Martha were
also entrusted to Captain Edmondson. With the exception
of some wild seas and sailing dangerously close to some
'white water' near the outer reef of an island one night, of
which the passengers fortunately were blissfully ignorant,
the next few weeks were uneventful, until one morning the
captain announced they were now sailing parallel to the
coast of the great southern continent. Jane peered in vain
for some sight of land, but in the interests of safety, Captain
Edmondson sailed well clear. Sailors stated that the southern
coastline accorded spectacular scenery, but also that it had
a treacherous reputation, and already had claimed many
vessels as they approached Port Phillip. Low-lying reefs and
sections of cliff face which had broken away had proven fatal
to many ships.

Chapter Five

SOME DAYS LATER THERE WAS A CRY FROM THE BOATSWAIN aloft that a ship was ahead. An order was given to take in sail, and shortly after the *Esperance* slackened pace, a school of whales sped past, leaving behind a tremendous wake and tossing the passengers about in the artificial swell. There was no time to admire or fear these magnificent creatures because directly behind, in hot pursuit, came a longboat. It's support vessel, a whaling ship, could just be seen in the distance. The smaller craft was travelling so fast that it appeared to be in tow, which in fact was revealed, as it approached the *Esperance*. The sea was red with blood and the longboat slackened pace, as the wounded creature gave up the fight. Secured harpoons were clearly visible as the crippled mammal fought, weakly thrusting its body about. However, there was no time for the whalers to observe a rarely seen passing ship – it was concentration and all hands on deck as they battled with their prey.

All eyes were observing this fascinating exercise when suddenly without warning the spectators on deck saw a second whale heading with tremendous speed towards the small longboat and the now dead captive. Malcolm, the first mate, shouted, *'They're done for, they've killed a calf.'* Before the horrified onlookers, the enraged mother charged at the small craft, lashing it with her great tail and splintering the timbers before their eyes. Like a toy, the vessel was tossed high in the air, spewing the helpless occupants into the surrounding red sea. The whaling support vessel was far too distant to be of use.

Quick as a flash, Malcolm and the boatswain Davy lowered the *Esperance*'s lifeboat and rowed desperately towards the drowning men, sparing no thought for their own welfare. Of the four on board the whaleboat, only three were rescued. While they plucked a badly injured sailor out of the water, another hauled himself aboard. The headman, clinging to a piece of timber was also rescued, revealing an injured leg. When the safety boat was alongside the *Esperance*, the passengers looked on in horror, as if unable to believe what they had just witnessed. Malcolm explained that the disaster had occurred because the whalers had accidentally harpooned a calf, and as with most animals, a mother protecting her young is far more dangerous than the wildest bull. Malcolm estimated that they were probably some 20 miles from the whaling station, and after considerable difficulty raising the injured men, sails were hoisted and they set off towards one of the few habitations along this desolate coastline.

Signals were exchanged with the whaling ship, which fortunately, like the *Esperance*, remained unscathed. Appreciative that their injured men were being cared for and returned to their remote coastal settlement, the whaling ship sailed on till the carcase, their source of income, was salvaged. It was then secured and towed to the station for processing.

The entire operation seemed to have taken a long time, and eventually, as the sun was setting behind them, they saw land in the distance. Either side of the whaling cove the cliffs looked rugged and uninviting, with no possible approach. Yet this one small sheltered bay broke the monotony of the towering cliffs along the rest of the coastline. The site seemed ideally located. The half moon bay had a high hill as a backdrop, providing an excellent lookout, while a shallow river flowed into the sea on the western side, ensuring abundant fresh water and fish. Between the hill and the river were several dwellings where the inhabitants obviously lived, while the eastern half of the cove housed sheds for treating the carcases and extracting their oil. Beyond the dwellings, a few sheep and cattle grazed. Even before the ship had anchored, one could smell the stench from the treating works. To Jane's surprise, the figures of three women in long dresses could be clearly distinguished on the beach, their hands raised to their foreheads straining to see, as if in anticipation of bad news. The *Esperance* anchored in the harbour while Malcolm and Davy rowed the stricken whalers ashore.

Throughout the proceedings, passengers stared curiously at this first glimpse of their new country. It certainly looked very different from their homeland. The sandy beach, river and foreshore appeared welcoming enough, but the country in the hinterland seemed to be densely wooded and rather forbidding. Alistair and Jane were curious to hear details of the settlers upon Malcolm's return.

It was late at night before the splash of oars sounded as Malcolm and Davy approached in the safety boat. No thought of sailing before daybreak was considered. During his years as a whaler, Malcolm had visited several whaling stations, but never this one. He pronounced the natural surroundings of the inlet as ideal. The headman was a Yorkshire man who had been transported to Van Diemen's Land for a minor offence. After gaining a pardon, he had no desire to return to England, so instead had set himself up at this site, and brought his wife and children here. Some of his children had left, but he still had one son, who was one of the lucky young men who survived. Two of the women on the beach were the headman's wife and daughter, the third being the wife of the man who had drowned that afternoon. Malcolm had tried to persuade the headman to accompany the *Esperance* to Sydney and get treatment for his damaged leg, but he refused to leave his family. Malcolm felt that in time he would be able to hobble with the aid of a crutch but his whaling days were definitely over. He seemed undaunted nevertheless, and with his son as support, the headman believed that other whalers would call and he would have sufficient men to operate his station, and that the proceeds of the oil would continue to provide them with adequate funds. The other injured sailor was battered and bruised, but thankfully his injuries were not serious. To Jane it seemed a remote and unrewarding existence.

The whalers obviously had scoured the coastline thoroughly before selecting this site, which was sheltered and ideal for their purpose with its lookout on the hill. As the *Esperance* sailed once more into the open sea, it was clear that sheer cliffs on either side of the cove offered little refuge for any vessel. Even though the weather was calm, the passengers could see huge waves pounding the perilous cliffs relentlessly. An error of judgement here would ensure instant disaster. Malcolm explained to Alistair that the station was well equipped and the headman's wife told them many ships called there, as it offered a haven after the harsh southern seas, where more and more whalers were venturing in search of their prey. The headman's wife told Malcolm that she and her daughter had travelled to Port Phillip, Sydney and even up to Moreton Bay with her husband. Their contact with people from inland was negligible, however many passing ships called, providing them with sufficient communication to meet their limited needs.

It was reassuring for Jane and Alistair to know they were adjacent to the southern continent, yet there would be no more sightings of land until they approached Port

Phillip Bay. The coastline, although charted, still posed many dangers, and even though it was now late spring in the southern hemisphere, storms still blew up with very little warning and Captain Edmondson took no chances. He felt confident of his seamanship on the open water, and believed the only risks beyond his control were from storms blowing the *Esperance* onto rocks and sandbars, or sailing into hidden reefs. These disasters occurred when you sailed too close to the coast, so almost three weeks passed before land was sighted. The sun shone brightly every day. A stronger sun than they had known in Scotland. The wind dropped and their progress was slower. As it became hotter, the stuffiness and smells below decks were once more unpleasant, but they were still not as vile as when they had crossed the equator.

A couple with small children were an inspiration to Jane. The young mother of three looked as well as anyone on board. Every day their father wandered round, often with the 2 and 4 year olds tied to him with a piece of rope, while Julia, his wife, nursed their baby, playing with him in a loving and joyous way, just as if she were at home. Julia told Jane that she had never seen so much of her husband since they had married. Usually, he left for work at daybreak and returned home late in the evening. Since their voyage, her husband had seen more of his young family than ever before and so they loved their passage. The different way people looked at trials inspired Jane. She felt the attitude of this young couple was excellent and their appearance reflected it. Captain

Edmondson also looked well, but then he loved the sea, this was his life and he appeared to have enjoyed every day since leaving Scotland, including the storms. Several passengers, on the other hand, were showing obvious signs of illness and Jane wondered how they would cope with the demands placed on them in this foreign land. It was something to be thankful for that both she and Alistair were well. It was also a relief to know she was not pregnant. Jane had hoped this would be the case at least until they arrived at their destination.

Chapter Six

EVEN BEFORE THE COAST WAS SIGHTED THERE WAS A CRY of '*Land ahoy*' as, after weeks at sea, people observed unfamiliar birds and smelt the new vegetation. The relief on the faces of passengers, knowing that a perilous ordeal had been survived, was enormous. Some even seemed lighthearted despite cold and bracing winds on deck.

After sailing through a narrow headland, every possible vantage point was taken as the entrance expanded and the *Esperance* sailed towards its destination. On either side of the bay, beautiful sandy beaches stretched in front of green wooded hills in the background. It was very scenic. Closer to the township, the Williamstown Lighthouse stood out as a welcoming landmark. One couldn't observe much from the *Esperance*, but it was clearly an established settlement offering welcome civilisation, even if basic, following months at sea. After the treacherous conditions of the Southern Ocean and the icy winds and dark, snow-bound days of Scotland, Port Phillip in late November was welcoming. In fact, it was not southern winters which were talked about, rather the scorching summers, which brought droughts, dust, hot winds, and worst of all, bushfires. Beyond the sandy beaches the countryside looked quite flat with the exception of some green hills sloping towards darker mountains in the distance. The verdure here was not the green of home, while foliage appeared a bluish grey.

The *Esperance* came some way up a river before docking at a wharf. There was a scramble among some of the passengers to get ashore as soon as possible. Collecting their modest possessions, Jane packed them into Ewan's trunk and waited patiently. During the afternoon, she had made a point of saying goodbye to passengers they had come to know well during the last three months. When, if ever, they might meet again, who knew? Finally, with mixed emotions they farewelled their home of the past months and thanked Captain Edmondson, Malcolm and Davy, grateful for their seamanship, caution and judgement, a trait manifested on numerous occasions. The seamen shook Alistair's hand and hugged his lovely young wife. The tall masts looked majestic and the vessel stately, but not all that robust to have sailed so far and endured mountainous seas. Jane gave a little prayer of thanks as they disembarked at Queen's Wharf in preparation for a new life together in this unknown colony. A few passengers were continuing to Sydney, but before setting sail, wool, grain and other produce was to be loaded for shipment to England.

Several passengers hired carts lined up beside a

warehouse to transport their trunks and other possessions, however in one instance it was all to no avail. Heavy rain had recently fallen, causing the wheels to get hopelessly bogged in mud. Several men unloaded the cart, pushed it out of the bog and carried the baggage some distance before reloading. Other women and children waited, guarding their possessions, as the men went in search of accommodation. Alistair dragged Ewan's trunk, with the tent tied to it, behind him, but thoughtfully a young lad helped him load it onto his cart with another family's baggage, enabling Jane and Alistair to trek towards the settlement, with other emigrants, behind the wagon.

A large parkland adjacent to the new township and not too far from the river displayed numerous tents. Amongst the native gums, English trees had been planted, in stark contrast to local flora, so that young oaks and elms offered an unexpected familiarity. The tents were lined with bricks to withstand rough weather. They had been provided by the Governor of New South Wales. A small fee covered one month's stay, until other arrangements could be established. With so many new settlers arriving, Captain Charles La Trobe was endeavouring to oversee the orderly establishment of the Port Phillip District, recently named Melbourne. Although vastly different from Scotland, the environment, to Jane, did not seem foreign. Scottish accents could be heard, and everywhere a sense of enthusiasm prevailed. Rather than feeling overwhelmed at the prospect ahead, a positivity emanated from the locals. The creation of this southern hemisphere settlement appeared exciting, not daunting.

After accepting assistance to assemble their tent, Jane and Alistair stowed away their belongings and set out to explore the area. Arm in arm they walked along a path towards the river, admiring the strange flora and fauna. It was so different to their homeland. Joining two young lads staring up a tree, they saw their first native animal, a koala perched above, nibbling leaves. They then crossed a muddy road with pedestrians, horse riders and carriages, before reaching the river. It was a pleasing sight, wide and fast flowing. They sat on the bank and rested while observing the intermittent activity of small rowing boats. A narrow wooden footbridge existed for pedestrians, but nothing for carriages. Plans were afoot for the construction of a bridge, so a passer-by informed them. As he was clearly a local, Alistair enquired if he might know the whereabouts of Hugh Mortimer's residence. Luck was with them – it was east of the township centre, and not far from the immigrant camp.

Whilst not keen to convey Ewan's tragic tidings, the discharge of his entrusted money could not come soon enough. Throughout their journey, Alistair had gone to great lengths to keep it safely concealed. The MacLeays' money from Archie was stowed in Jane's corset. Afraid to leave Ewan's English pounds unguarded in their tent, Alistair had stowed them in a satchel slung across his shoulders. Returning to their tent, they agreed that to carry Ewan's trunk was impossible. Alistair packed Ewan's personal effects into a sack, which he strapped to his back, while the English pounds remained in the satchel across his shoulder.

Just as they set off, it commenced raining heavily, turning the streets to mud. After a damp walk, they reached the Mortimers' timber residence. It was an impressive home which included stables and a side garden, orchard and vegetable patch. Standing at the front door, Jane was conscious of her dirty shoes and muddy petticoat. Just as she was attempting to clean her boots on the grass, a young girl opened the front door and ushered them into a drawing room where a window overlooked the street. Before an open fire a middle-aged man stood. He greeted them genially, directing them to a couch opposite the fireplace, however there was about him an air of apprehension, as if suspecting danger or bad news, a sensation to which people often succumbed when ships arrived with tidings from their homeland.

In a simple manner Alistair reported the fate of their dear friend Ewan, recounting his popularity with fellow travellers and their fondness of him. He then handed over the papers entrusted to him, and Ewan's personal belongings. Mr Mortimer listened in silence, remaining seated for some time before ringing a bell. A young maid appeared, listened to his request, and then returned with brandy, at which point Ewan's uncle promptly excused himself. Sometime later, he returned with his wife. Mr Mortimer was clearly shattered and barely spoke thereafter. His wife, Georgina, after expressing her shock and sorrow, enquired about Jane and Alistair's circumstances and their plans in the colony. Mindful of her husband's present distress, she suggested Jane and Alistair might perhaps leave, but if they could return for dinner tomorrow evening, that would be appreciated? Graciously the visitors accepted, but before departing, Alistair stated there was one further matter. Removing the satchel from his shoulder, he extracted what was to the MacLeays a small fortune, and handed it to Hugh Mortimer, at the same time, recounting Ewan's instructions.

A profound silence ensued. Eventually, Georgina Mortimer arose, and after thanking them sincerely, she extended both hands in an appreciative gesture, reiterating tomorrow's dinner invitation. Communicating with her husband in his present state would not be sensible. For Alistair and Jane, the following night would open up a new and unexpected horizon.

Ewan's death was a shattering blow to Hugh Mortimer. His future in the colony depended on Ewan's management of his Murray River station, ensuring long-term production of wool, and regular shipments to the family's Yorkshire mill. Hugh had invested significant sums of money into the property in preparation for Ewan's arrival. Profound shock overwhelmed him.

Equally extraordinary was the trusted conveyance of such a sizeable sum of money from his brother. Clearly Henry in

Yorkshire was as passionate about the venture as he was. The likelihood of the average emigrant delivering what to them would be a fortune, was inconceivable. After Ewan's death, no family members would have even known that he had died, let alone any details. The funds could have disappeared within this country, or gone to America. It was unbelievable. That these fine young Scots had faithfully complied with Ewan's wishes and delivered his possessions, including a sizeable sum of money, was nothing short of a miracle. As to when Ewan actually left England, and on which vessel, his relatives had no idea, whilst the task of tracing the captain and his ship would have been like looking for a needle in a haystack. Georgina, too, was in disbelief, but unlike her husband, she was managing to function. Providence had struck an appalling blow, but was there, perhaps hope? Might it be possible for this couple to take over their nephew's role? At least one thing was certain. They could be trusted!

In expectation of supplying wool to his brother's Yorkshire mill, Hugh Mortimer had invested in a sizeable tract of land along the Murray River, which his nephew, Ewan, had agreed to manage. Jack Henderson, a client of Hugh Mortimer's, owned a neighbouring station. Observation of Henderson's profits from both wool and timber was the motive behind Mortimer's investment. It was the venture about which Ewan had excitedly spoken. Presently 500 cattle and several horses grazed there, but in anticipation of Ewan's arrival, his uncle had availed himself of a tempting deal and purchased 1,000 sheep from a station south-west of Sydney. That large mob was presently en route to Mirrimbali, the river property. JimJim, an Aboriginal boy, and Gideon, a pardoned convict, temporarily managed the run. So it was not only the shock of Ewan's death but also the consequence of it that had shattered Hugh Mortimer. Their futures had been bound together.

To Hugh and Georgina, it gradually became apparent that, while nothing could replace the tragic loss of their nephew, providence, after all, might take care of them. Here was a charming couple and the young man's background was farming; they had departed Scotland under desperate circumstances, with no foreseeable occupation in the colony. Without their presence at Ewan's tragic death, the likelihood of the Mortimers ever receiving Henry's sizeable contribution was remote; hence their integrity! What was their honesty worth? The answer was obvious, but whether it would be accepted, remained to be seen. So with encouragement from his wife, Hugh Mortimer proposed to Alistair and Jane that they take over Ewan's role and settle at Mirrimbali Station on the Murray River. As a reward for their honest conduct and as a long-term incentive, a section of land with river frontage would be allotted to the MacLeays. With few options, Alistair and Jane most likely would have accepted this offer regardless, but the inducement of their own property, especially alongside a river in this hot arid land, was an enticement beyond their expectations. Equally, as Georgina emphasised to her husband, it had been in

Ewan's interest, as a significant beneficiary, to do all he could to ensure the success of the venture. No one else had that motivation, hence the bestowal of land. And so, without Ewan and with the imminent arrival of 1,000 sheep, it was in the Mortimer family's best interests to secure a reliable manager as soon as possible and here he was, with a loving wife to support him.

After dinner with the Mortimers, Jane and Alistair were offered accommodation with friends of their hosts who owned a farm not too far from the settlement in an area called Heidelberg, where they enjoyed walks along a nearby river. A bountiful orchard, vegetable garden, dairy, chicken and pig pens comprised this productive property, beside the fast-flowing Yarra River. The farm was established on a large scale and its produce was a very welcome supply to both new and longer-term settlers. Grateful for the accommodation, Alistair and Jane rolled up their sleeves and contributed where they could. Alistair helped his host convey food to a stall at a weekly market, where all the produce sold very swiftly.

Time spent with the cultivated Mortimers and their friends had temporarily reassured Jane, but the prospect of their journey ahead, combined with an unknown life in what people called 'the outback', caused mild apprehension. The additional knowledge that she might now be pregnant added to her unease.

In addition to acquiring sheep, Hugh Mortimer had

offered the drovers Keith Brown and his son Billy, who were driving the mob down, somewhere to live and payment, if they could remain at Mirrimbali Station for a few extra months. Gideon and JimJim had been managing the cattle and overseeing other chores, but since sheep were to be the principal investment, it therefore, was essential that someone with knowledge and expertise could oversee their breeding, wool clipping and maintenance. Another issue was the impossibility of fencing and keeping the herd on the station. It was hoped that, by reason of acreage, there would be ample food, even in a drought, but keeping track of the mob would require shepherds. The river was one boundary, but to ensure the flock did not stray, Keith and Billy agreed to rotate overnight watches with Gideon and JimJim. With no other work, an offer of both accommodation and wages was too good to refuse. The drover and his son had happily agreed to remain till the sheep were shorn and for the first breeding season. In Scotland, natural hedges and ancient stone fences provided boundaries, but in this arid colony, constructing barriers for stock was more challenging.

As well as meeting Jack Henderson, originally from Sydney, who had directed Hugh to the very desirable river frontage station adjacent to his property, Amaru, Hugh Mortimer had experienced another unusual piece of good fortune. On their voyage to the colony in 1839, as upper deck passengers, the captain had drawn to Hugh's attention a young lad, Charlie Chester, who had come aboard as a stowaway. In fear of being transported to Van Diemen's Land for stealing chickens, which he had done to provide food for his widowed mother and starving siblings, the boy had fled authorities, stowing away on board a vessel, which he imagined was sailing to America. Terrified when first discovered, he was fortunate to face a compassionate captain, who after hearing his narrative, did not react harshly but instead believed the most effective recourse was to engage him as an extra crew member, since no fare had been paid. Quickly Charlie learned to adjust sails and respond to weather conditions, but it was his talent for solving problems and repairing damage that was quickly recognised, not only by the captain, but all the crew. Nothing seemed beyond this creative stowaway's talent. Employed by his uncle in the construction industry, Charlie had become a gifted and creative builder. On arrival in the colony, the Mortimers provided accommodation for Charlie, while he, in turn, was paid to build their home. It was a mutually beneficial arrangement. Then, after purchasing the river run and arranging for his English nephew to manage it, Hugh again engaged Charlie, to relocate up to his Murray River property where he was required to build a homestead, shearing shed and stockyards. Charlie had married the daughter of immigrants who had settled in Melbourne. A fine frontier woman, Anna accompanied her husband inland. Building materials were loaded onto a bullock wagon and Hugh Mortimer travelled with Charlie and his wife to Mirrimbali Station.

Comprehending his master's requirements and trusting him, Charlie commenced work with enthusiasm. Under his instructions, both Gideon and JimJim contributed, while learning a great deal about building. They continued to oversee cows, chickens and goats and established an orchard and vegetable garden. With produce and diverse animals, the station was self-supporting. Anna and Charlie loved the environment and in turn learned a great deal from Gideon and JimJim. One memorable experience was the opportunity to view a passing Aboriginal tribe perform a Corrobboree. In the company of JimJim, Charlie and Gideon were privileged witnesses.

Charlie managed to build some log railings on the boundary of the property stretching down to the river. Gideon and JimJim endeavoured to copy Charlie's log barrier, but it was impossible to fence in the vast run. They did, however, plant native bushes as a hedge for quite some distance. It grew haphazardly, and while not in the class of beautiful English hedgerows, it did form a boundary, albeit an illusory one, which did not fool the savvy stock. Both sheep and cattle penetrated it, but any deterrent was useful, especially when there was plenty of green pasture. Charlie and his wife loved Mirrimbali and would willingly have remained a bit longer, but once the homestead, shed, shearers' quarters and stockyards were built, they returned to Melbourne, where more immigrants were regularly arriving and work was in demand.

Chapter Seven

After a couple of weeks, Hugh Mortimer advised the MacLeays that he had contacted a carrier, who with his bullock wagon would transport them to Mirrimbali, his Murray River station. Hugh planned to return to the northern river district shortly. Although the teamster's wagon was loaded with supplies for the inland journey, the dray could accommodate Alistair and Jane. Delivery of mail between the central Post Office and the newly settled Murray River township was also the carrier's task. When they arrived at the settlement, transport to Mirrimbali would be arranged.

Hugh Mortimer gave Alistair a letter for Jack Henderson, advising of the tragic loss of his nephew and introducing the MacLeays. If Jack and Miriam, his wife, could offer any support and encouragement to Mirrimbali's new residents as they adjusted to their unfamiliar and remote terrain, Hugh would be eternally grateful.

As anticipated, the trek to their new home was arduous, but their teamster, Clarence, although rough and ready, was a considerate chap and respectful of Jane. Habitation along the route was primitive, but the Cobdens' tent stood them in good stead. Luckily the journey was uneventful. At least, unlike on other continents, wild animals were not a threat, although they had been warned to be on the lookout for snakes. After their recent Highlands trek, it was with wonderment that they viewed the distinctive colonial countryside. Even with one's eyes closed, you knew you were not in Scotland – the sounds, smells and temperature were entirely different. Initially the terrain was mountainous, but after crossing what Clarence referred to as the Great Dividing Range, the countryside changed into extensive plains. The further north they travelled, the drier and dustier the pastures became.

Alistair loved studying the native flora, pointing out different plants to Jane. Even the extensive gum trees varied in their formation. Kangaroos and wallabies jumping through the scrub were particularly fascinating, while the various bird calls were very different from Scotland. Crows and magpies had their unique quarks, but flocks of white cockatoos, swooping round the landscape with their constant cries, as if in conversation, absorbed Alistair. The odd, detached wombat occasionally waddled across their path as well.

The plains lacked the diversity of the mountains but it was smoother and easier travelling. Jane's entire life had been spent only within the precinct of Kirkfeldy, so this journey revealed such a different world. Like observant Alistair, she loved the colonial countryside and its unique wildlife, but from a scenic perspective, there was no comparison to the breathtaking views of Scotland.

Eventually, after several days, they reached the river settlement. Like other inhabited sites en route, it was primitive, but a redeeming feature was the vast river flowing beside a small cottage where Clarence deposited them. Observing their arrival, a kind lady greeted them and offered to mind their baggage, as they looked for a suitable place to assemble their tent. Young men sawing felled gum trees at an adjacent timber yard, caused significant noise, while a small boat could be seen moored along the river bank. There was evidence of constructive activity everywhere. Clarence was warmly thanked, before he lead his trusty nags down a wooded embankment to the river, where they were hobbled and free to roam, but not too far. It was a picturesque site, but pitching their tent under numerous gum trees did not seem wise to Alistair, especially as the wind was strong. So they set off to find a suitable location.

However, before the young couple had even commenced their inspection of this barely settled village, they were approached by a young man, who had been instructed to convey them to Mirrimbali Station. Both were enthusiastic, until the fellow explained that it would be sensible to come now, since the punt would shortly cross the river, enabling them to reach the station today. Jane was very disappointed, having assumed their new home would be on the south side of the river near the settlement. That the only access to civilian life would entail crossing the river by punt was, to her, a very real handicap. Alistair, however, remained positive, confident that, knowing Hugh Mortimer, his property would be safe and productive. He reminded Jane of the various rivers, albeit not so large, in Scotland, and their journey across Loch Ness. As he correctly divined, a small boat for river navigation was moored at Mirrimbali. Although it entailed rowing against the current, the settlement was in fact closer via the river than on horseback along a winding dusty track. With mixed emotions, they climbed aboard the wagon and set off for their new life.

Awaiting them at Mirrimbali were Gideon and JimJim. Living in the homestead they had helped Charlie build, the lads were expecting Mr Mortimer's nephew, so Alistair and Jane's arrival gave them quite a surprise. But they instantly warmed to the young Scots. A sleep-out on the back veranda was all the lads had required, but now with the MacLeays in residence, Gideon and JimJim chose to move into the nearby shearers' quarters which Charlie had built behind the shed.

Mirrimbali was certainly above and beyond the MacLeays' expectations. A long driveway lined with young oaks eventually revealed stockyards and a shed with accommodation for shearers and other workers at the rear. This approach to the property was impressive, however, when the road arched round to the right exposing a circular lawn and a gracious homestead on one side, with grass sloping down to a bend in the river on the other, Alistair and

Jane's breath was taken away. They did not know which way to look! A wide veranda with large windows in a gracious homestead was one thing, but spectacular views across the grass to the river were remarkable. This surely was a unique location in this sparse dry land. The river was exceptional, but for the homestead to actually overlook superb views both up and downstream reinforced the reality that Mirrimbali Station had been established on a truly rare site. This was definitely on a par with Scottish lochs.

That the new arrivals were very impressed was obvious to Gideon and JimJim. Their bags were barely deposited before they set off down to the river to admire the spectacular scenery. Nothing could have prepared them for this setting. Jane had been disappointed that Mirrimbali was on the north side of the river, but as they observed the landscape, the reason became abundantly clear. The land where the homestead was located on the north side was high, with remarkable views and no risk of flooding, whereas the opposite side, while densely wooded, was low-lying for miles and definitely would be subject to water inundation, should the river ever rise.

Gideon explained that the state of Victoria recently had been established south of the river, while the northern side remained as New South Wales, and the Port Phillip District, now named Melbourne, was the capital and independent from Sydney.

When Jane walked back from the riverbank to the

homestead, she didn't go inside to unpack, but instead remained on the veranda, walking up and down, absorbing the extraordinary views of the Murray River as it wound across the countryside. Compared to the dry land with sparse vegetation which they had observed while journeying north, this certainly was an exceptional setting and not what she or Alistair anticipated. Scotland, of course, had beautiful lochs, but none were near Kirkfeldy.

Observing Gideon and JimJim collecting their possessions in the rear room, Jane said that she and Alistair would be very happy for them to remain in the homestead, but the lads preferred their independence and chose the shearers' quarters.

Gideon was an emancipated convict from Van Diemen's Land. Seized by the demon drink, he had been transported for theft, despite having no recollection of his actual crime when found yet again in a drunken state on the streets of Manchester. During the long sea voyage, Reverend Mills, a Presbyterian minister passionate about reforming convicts, many of whom were transported for minor offences or had little education and stole for survival, had arranged basic lessons every day for these unfortunate lawbreakers. For Gideon, it proved to be an awakening, which brought about a life-changing transformation in him. Skills he had learned as a young boy were encouraged, helping him realise he could be a worthwhile person. When he assisted Charlie Chester to build Mr Mortimer's homestead, his confidence, especially with carpentry, was further enhanced. That he could have died in his late teens or been imprisoned for life was never far from Gideon's mind, and so with that awareness, and unforgettable memories of Port Arthur, came an acceptance that regrettably, unlike other people, it would never again be possible for him to imbibe.

Gideon was both a good companion and role model for JimJim. The latter had learned to ride on the Mortimer station and loved the thrill of horseback motion. He was a fine specimen of a man, tall, lean and fit. Shortly after his association with Mirrimbali and friendship with Gideon, JimJim's mother had died. Rather than moving on with his tribe, JimJim chose to remain with Gideon on the station. Both as a companion and a useful helper with construction, Gideon valued JimJim's support, while the latter learned skills with cattle, carpentry and communication in English. Gideon was a patient and reliable mentor. Both boys were well remunerated by Hugh Mortimer in appreciation of their hard work and dependability.

Although Jane and Alistair's new home was remote, they valued that it was beside the spectacular, wide and fast-flowing Murray River. That it was safe from flooding and offered superb views across the water to an extensive native forest were huge factors. Naturally, it was isolated and lonely, but to Jane there was something calming and therapeutic about overlooking water. The community was limited in this remote location, but the few settlers, naturally, were there for each other.

Until Hugh Mortimer arrived, they could not be sure which allotment had been assigned to them, but it seemed apparent that land overlooking the river to the north-west would be theirs.

Hearing of their arrival, Jack Henderson, the Mirrimbali neighbour, rode across to the property and introduced himself. Alistair handed him their letter of introduction. Mirrimbali was set on a large U-bend in the river occupying a sizeable stretch of land with views both up and downstream. Jack's neighbouring station, Amaru, occupied land along the river upstream, which meant Jane and Alistair's allocated land must therefore be downstream towards the west. The source of the Murray, Jack relayed, was in the Snowy Mountains and it flowed across to the Coorong at Encounter Bay on the southern coast. As Highland Scots, neither of the MacLeays had ever learned to swim, but Jack Henderson was adamant that Alistair must acquire this skill. During the hot summer, Jack regularly rode to Mirrimbali and accompanied Alistair down to the sandbank, where with patience and encouragement he learned the art of safely swimming across the river. Although terrified at first, Alistair, with the security of Jack beside him, gradually learned to tread water near the edge, where it was still possible to stand. Alistair soon overcame his fear, valuing how refreshing it was to cool down in the river on hot days and, last but not least, he learned to respect the dangerous current. Jack's wise counsel was, *'When crossing the river, if caught in a current, you must never panic, but instead quietly float and between rests, gradually swim towards the bank. How far downstream you drift is not a problem, since you can always walk back along the sandbank. The worse thing is to panic and fight the current.'*

By the end of the summer Alistair was a confident swimmer, ensuring the two neighbours enjoyed many special times swimming together in the fast-flowing stream. Gideon and JimJim also learned to swim and navigate the river. They were invaluable to their new resident. Although Alistair had extensive knowledge and experience of farming, the conditions in southern New South Wales were considerably different from the Highlands. Sometimes, just seeking their opinion made all the difference. In turn, the two lads loved and respected the new residents.

Hugh Mortimer's intention to fund the property so that it functioned as efficiently as possible was also a huge plus. Charlie had adapted a plough and, using bullocks to drag a sharp metal scoop over the soil, showed Gideon and JimJim how, by excavating a substantial area of land, a dam could be created. Once shown how to do it, the pair became enthusiastic contributors. Charlie also created a clever wheel pump in the river. Lead pipes were connected to a circular wooden frame, set higher up on the bank. Harnessed bullocks or horses, when set in motion, caused the wheel to rotate, bringing water up through the pipes to the nearby dam. Never having seen such a mechanism, Alistair was mesmerised. That water from the river could be channelled to the dam, and then to the orchard and vegetable garden, was extraordinary. Charlie must be a truly gifted and clever young man.

Mostly the system functioned. As well as being useful, the dam was aesthetically pleasing, with tall reeds surrounding it. However, towards the end of autumn, when minimal rain had fallen and the river level had dropped, the dam started turning into a brown muddy quagmire. In good seasons, though, channels were dug from the dam to the home paddock to irrigate trees in the orchard and maintain the vegetable garden. Rainfall in the Scottish Highlands was such that these measures had never been necessary. Life in this arid land was entirely different.

Two dogs, Red and Ringo, guarded the property, while chickens dwelt in a logged off area adjacent to the shed, where Gideon hoped they would be safe from roaming eagles. Without the protection of their aggressive rooster, the hens had no hope of survival. Even the dogs were wary of the rooster.

Gradually Alistair and Jane adapted to their new environment, but cold dark nights in June and July still seemed strange, while stifling heat and twilight till 8 pm in January seemed even more extraordinary. Used to a white Christmas with snow as far as the eye could see, they needed to adjust to the scorching summer heat in January and

February. However, it appeared that northern hemisphere Christmas traditions were maintained in the colony, with roast turkey, ham and plum pudding the typical fare. Hugh Mortimer had arranged for seedlings to be brought from England in the hope of establishing crops. Among them were acorns, which the lads had planted, so that small oaks formed an avenue from the property entrance to the homestead. Whether these young trees might grow, as in the old country, remained to be seen.

Hugh Mortimer had developed the property in a thorough and efficient manner. Fortunate as he was to have the resources to do so, he had stinted on nothing, and made few mistakes. The homestead was exceptional. That the Mortimer family would occasionally stay there was one factor, but Hugh's main consideration had been that the property would be acceptable and appealing to his nephew. On board the *Esperance,* Ewan had shared that he planned to remain in the colony for several years, but Hugh Mortimer's expectation of his nephew's commitment was clearly much longer, hence the quality and importance of all construction. The supply and export of wool to his brother's successful mill in England was his long-term objective.

Mirrimbali was a gracious colonial homestead. A sitting room and dining room located on the right of the front door provided views across the wide grass area which stretched down to the extensive river bend, as it wound its way through the country. To the left of the front door was a large bedroom which also benefited from this beautiful view. A kitchen was on the east side. Two bedrooms and a study at the rear faced north. Contrary to Scottish perspective where winter sun streamed from the south, the rear rooms were bathed in winter sunlight from the north. All the living quarters had open fireplaces.

The homestead was far more spacious and comfortable than any Scottish home Alistair and Jane had ever seen. Castles, of course, had been visited, but that was not normal living. A wash-house abutted the kitchen, while the outhouse was located some distance between the shed and the back door. In addition to the outhouse, a commode was placed in each bedroom. Overall, it was far more comfortable than anything they ever had experienced in the Highlands, and it certainly exceeded their expectations of life in New South Wales.

Chapter Eight

Months passed quickly after the MacLeays settled at Mirrimbali and Jane's pregnancy advanced. Fortunately, she had been well throughout and became anxious only as the birth approached. Miriam Henderson recommended a nurse who had delivered numerous babies in the outback. Although she presently worked as a midwife near the goldfields at Sandhurst, Miriam was sure she would travel north to assist. Within weeks, a confirming letter preceded the arrival of Nurse Thorne, who settled into Alistair and Jane's home.

Just one week later, thankfully without too much distress, Alexander Sinclair MacLeay arrived, known from day one as Sandy. Despite sleepless nights and round the clock attention, his arrival brought much joy. The support of Nurse Thorne for a couple of weeks was invaluable. Even though Jane had managed Duncan from birth, she lacked confidence and appreciated Nurse Thorne's expert knowledge and guidance for both herself and baby Sandy.

Although it had not been without difficulties and huge

adjustments, Alistair and Jane were very grateful for their New South Wales life. Unlike many migrants, they felt safe, and although tenants, they were financially secure. That a small section of land with river frontage actually belonged to them was a fiscal surety they had never expected. In quick succession after Sandy's arrival, three additional siblings joined him. They had four wonderful healthy children. The young sons and daughters loved their rural environment and assisted their father in simple ways.

Initially visitors were rare, but after Captain Cadell crossed the Coorong in his cleverly designed boat the *Lady Augusta* and navigated the Murray up to Albury, paddle steamers, sometimes towing barges, frequently sailed past the station. If Mirrimbali residents were sighted, then a loud horn invariably sent forth a greeting.

Life on the land was familiar to Alistair, however, in this arid environment, skills were required for the management of Mirrimbali that he did not possess. That Hugh Mortimer had arranged for the drovers, Keith and Billy, after driving down the mob, to remain at Mirrimbali for the first lambing and shearing season, had been invaluable. It helped Alistair enormously. Lambing, crutching and shearing were challenging, but with Gideon and JimJim working as well, he learned a great deal. It didn't happen overnight, but gradually, knowledge and confidence were acquired. Once areas had been eaten down, the vast flock was moved on. Taking a lead from Charlie, log fences were built by Gideon and JimJim in a bid to enclose extra areas. In Scotland this task had been easier. Stone fences and hedges to separate animals on the MacLeays' farm had been in place for generations. And contrary to New South Wales, the climate in Kirkfeldy was such that water was plentiful and additional irrigation never was required. In preparation for droughts, Alistair endeavoured to absorb the skilful way Gideon had drained water from the man-made dam, via channels, extending water to outlying areas.

Annually Keith and Billy returned at shearing time, bringing a couple of extra lads to assist with the volume and train them. Ten years later, two of that original group still turned up at shearing time. Keith and Billy travelled on horseback from station to station and were well known in southern New South Wales.

For the first few years, the wool bales were loaded onto bullock wagons and carted to Echuca for the journey to Melbourne. But after navigation of the Murray, paddle steamers and barges became the most practical form of transport for wool, grain and timber. Station owners along the Darling and Murrumbidgee realised the river system was quicker and far less stressful than overland cartage to Sydney or Adelaide. The Port of Echuca was closer to the sea, namely Melbourne, than any other inland settlement.

Because only so many bales could fit on each cart, several trips via bullock wagon were required to deliver the station wool to Echuca. The road was long and circuitous and the punt had to be used to cross the river. To this end, it made sense to build a basic landing, where the wool could be loaded directly onto barges for shipment to the settlement. Bullock wagons then could transport the bales to Melbourne, prior to shipment to the Yorkshire mill. A Mirrimbali landing meant that guests, too, could visit via the river and other shipments could be conveyed simply. Gideon and JimJim possibly could have constructed the landing, but Charlie Chester was once again engaged and within weeks he arrived with construction equipment considerably more advanced than any available at Mirrimbali. And rather than saw logs, wood from a local timber yard was deposited at the sandbank. Just a few months later, the landing was completed. Soon wool, bagged and stored in the shearing shed, was loaded onto a barge for transfer to the settlement wharf, from where it went via bullock wagon to Melbourne.

Busy and occupied with their new life, time passed swiftly for Alistair and Jane. Sandy was a great joy and a wonderful older brother to three little siblings, who had joined him in quick succession, Charlotte, Thomas and Alicia. From day one, their youngest sister, Alicia, was simply Cis or Cissy. Initially, Charlotte and Thomas retained their proper names, until Alistair, in memory of his dear childhood friend, when affectionately summoning his sons for assistance, saddling horses or moving sheep would always call loudly, '*Sandy and "Tam", hurry up, boys, you're needed!*' Charlotte unsurprisingly became Lottie.

To assist Jane at this frenetic time, a young local girl was employed. Edith Quirk, just 14, came from the river settlement, Echuca, an Aboriginal word meaning 'meeting of the waters'. The Campaspe River flowed into the Murray at the town. Edith had virtually no education, her father having abandoned her mother before she was born. Not only was Edith's arrival appreciated by the entire MacLeay family, it was a reciprocal arrangement. In return, this virtual orphan was introduced to a way of life she most likely would never have known. Simple things, such as how to hold a knife and fork, to say nothing of reading, writing, courtesy and respect, were acquired. Fundamental principles and values demonstrated in this family would eventually enable Edith to have a life, which otherwise never would have been possible. The little MacLeays loved Edith's warm and loving response to them, ensuring she became part of their family.

Over the course of time, letters came from the Cobdens, as well as Archie and Martha. No word, however, was received from the Sinclairs. Although Alistair and Jane had been ostracised by James Sinclair, the neighbouring Highland community supported and admired the lovers who had fled to the southern hemisphere.

The MacLeay children grew up loving farm life with all its diverse attractions. At the age of 5, each child was taught to swim. Initially the instructions entailed simple dog-paddling. However, as they were surrounded by so much dangerous water, it was essential that in addition to learning to swim, basic principles about flowing water, whether rivers, dams or oceans, had to be engrained into each child. Number one was that you never swam alone, and number two was: never panic. Just quietly float or tread water; then, by taking time and remaining calm, one eventually reached the bank. Over the course of many years, few local people ever drowned in the river. When a tragic drowning did occur, it was invariably a visitor.

Despite her busy life, both in the homestead and on the property, Jane endeavoured to teach her children the alphabet, numbers and the basics of reading and writing. No schools existed until Sandy was 8, when two Irish sisters, Maeve and Eileen O'Donnell, arrived with their uncle and aunt. The O'Donnells had come to the colony as bounty passengers, single girls being very desirable, especially since the Gold Rush. Observing, upon their arrival, the need for education in the settlement, these sisters enthusiastically opened a little school called St Mary's. Sandy and Lottie were among the first pupils, followed in succession by Tam and Cissy. In no time, the two elder children had made great progress. The MacLeays warmed to the sisters straight away, thankful to have this nearby facility. As they settled in and extended the school, grateful parents contributed as much as they could to raise funds and assist. It was, nevertheless, quite a distance from Mirrimbali to and from school each day. Initially Gideon rowed the children upstream to the settlement, and then collected them at the end of the day.

Downstream he could pretty much let the current carry the boat using oars just for direction, but rowing against the current was far more taxing. Occasionally they rode their ponies to school, but it was a much longer trip.

A Scottish resident in the settlement was very critical of the MacLeays' schooling decision, by reason of the Irish Catholic influence. But Jane and Alistair were extremely grateful for the excellent education these two O'Donnell sisters provided, and that, combined with the wisdom of their beloved Scottish bard, Robbie Burns, ensured there were no concerns about religious influence – 'A Man's A Man For All That'! An open mind was what mattered, namely, who we are within.

Chapter Nine

With no prior notice, the MacLeays one day, unexpectedly, received some very welcome visitors. While reading to little Cissy who had been sick, Jane looked out the window and saw dust on the distant horizon near the entrance to Mirrimbali. Standing up to see more clearly, she soon made out two horsemen galloping down their long driveway towards the homestead. Alistair, Gideon and JimJim were working, she knew not where.

Leaving Cissy almost asleep, Jane opened the front door and crossed to the side of the veranda, where she could view the horsemen's approach more easily. Eventually the long driveway turned right leading directly to the homestead, but a timber gateway, designed to prevent stock from grazing in the immediate vicinity of the house, blocked access. To that end, Jane walked across the grass to greet the unknown arrivals and open the gate for them. Visitors were not common. Lottie and Tam continued playing in their sandpit, while Sandy raced across to join his mother.

Despite wearing a wide-brimmed hat, and 10 years

having passed since Jane last had seen her dearly loved brother, she instantly recognised Duncan, even before he dismounted. His companion remained in the saddle quietly observing the scene. Before Jane could open the gate, her brother leapt over it and threw himself into her arms. They hugged each other for several moments, before taking in the changes created by the passage of time and their respective worlds. It was one of those special lifetime experiences. Puzzled, Sandy stood by and watched. Then suddenly, before he knew what was happening, he was picked up and thrown in the air with great gusto, while being told affectionately in a strong Scottish accent, *'Oh Sandy, my bonnie buck, I have finally met you!'* Curiously Sandy did not feel at all frightened or apprehensive; he just wanted more fun and games, such as being thrown in the air by this exciting young man!

'How did you find us?' Jane asked. *'I did not know you were coming. It is surely a miracle that you are here!'* The dialogue could have continued for ages, but by then Lachlan Smith had dismounted and was standing beside them. Duncan introduced Jane. After years of hearing his friend speak incessantly of his sister, Lachlan felt as if he almost knew Jane. Now the height of his father, Duncan was a very handsome young man. Gathering up the pair from the sandpit, Jane, still in disbelief, went inside, checked Cissy and put the kettle on the stove. With a little boy following in their wake, Duncan and Lachlan unstrapped their bags and led the horses into the yards, before heading towards the homestead. Lachlan

carried the saddlebags, while Duncan hoisted Sandy onto his shoulders. Only a few minutes had passed, but already Sandy just adored his uncle!

Lachlan had relatives in Sydney, which was their next destination, but without Duncan, he never would have ventured to New South Wales, and so, however long his friend wished to remain on this station with his sister was fine with him. When Alistair walked in the back door and saw Duncan, he too was in disbelief. Having seen no friends or relatives since their elopement, the MacLeays were desperate for news of home and the Highlands in general. For Duncan, life at Kirkfeldy had never been the same since the departure of his sister. Hunter had felt remorse for his role in forcing Jane's return from her first elopement, but not so his father nor Walter. Gordon was not involved. Hunter with his wife Jeanie Macdonald had migrated to Philadelphia. Archie, Martha and their family were fine. Duncan had visited them before his voyage. At 18, with no thoughts of settling down and much adventure ahead, the two lads planned to visit Sydney before sailing to California. Although not sure how they would do it, they hoped to travel across the United States to visit Hunter in Philadelphia. Duncan was unsure as to where he wished to settle permanently, but one thing was certain, he would no longer live in Scotland. After visiting his siblings and seeing life in both countries, his future would become clear. Jane, Alistair and their children were a very strong attraction, making Duncan think that, ultimately, somewhere near them might be his verdict. Loved ones preceded location.

The two young Scots remained at Mirrimbali for several months and were of great assistance, especially during lambing. Duncan adored his little nieces and nephews and played endless games with them, including fun tricks and teasing, of which they never had enough. *'My turn now, my turn please, Dunks!'* were their endless cries. Unlike Jane, Duncan loved the voyage out and was not fearful. He could not swim but decided that if the vessel sank in the middle of the ocean, swimming would not be of much use anyway. He nevertheless watched in fascination and disbelief as the little MacLeay children swam with great confidence in the mighty Murray River. They were, of course, always in the company of adults, but their knowledge and self-assurance was such that, in the event they ever found themselves alone, they could calmly navigate the current and in due course reach the bank. Observing his sister's children swim with such confidence prompted Duncan to ask Alistair if he might teach him. After just a few days Duncan and Lachlan swam across the river to the southern bank. It was amazing! With great excitement the children joined them. Eventually, during their Sydney stay, the two young Scots were so pleased they had learned to swim, because the beautiful harbour with sunny beaches was the perfect setting to enjoy the sea, although by reason of huge waves, neither ventured out too far.

Watching these gorgeous little children play, and the

interaction with their parents, prompted Duncan to think of the joy his father might have derived had he allowed his daughter to marry her dearly loved suitor. Not much had changed at the Kirkfeldy cottage. His father and two brothers worked the same long hours, while a local girl cooked and cleaned for them.

Just before Duncan and Lachlan departed, a letter came from Hugh Mortimer to say that he, Georgina and their two daughters would be coming to stay within the next few days. Jane, with Edith's help, busily cleaned the homestead and relocated the entire family to the shearers' quarters with her brother and Lachlan.

Hugh and Georgina were appreciative and grateful for the way the MacLeays were managing Mirrimbali. Georgina, riding side-saddle, accompanied her husband as he inspected the station, but their daughters, Adelia and Alexandra, were not relaxed guests. Clearly country life was not their preference. Only once during their seven-day stay did they even venture down to the beautiful river. Other than meals in the dining room, they barely left the sitting room where they either read or worked on tapestries. Georgina wished to accompany her husband when he rode across to visit his old client, Jack Henderson, and his wife, Miriam. But Hugh, observing how rough the track was, decided a horse and cart would be safer. Riding, especially side-saddle, would be too hazardous for Georgina. The Mirrimbali horses were fine specimens, but most were wild and not properly trained.

Overall, Hugh Mortimer was very pleased with the way everything was being administered. The price of wool shipped to Yorkshire was excellent, but without Mirrimbali being run as it was, that income would cease. After observing the conditions in which the extended MacLeay family were residing in the shearers' quarters, instructions were given that a Manager's Cottage was to be built on the MacLeays' allotment, just a little further downstream. For Alistair and Jane, this was a massive bonus. Their own home! Always endeavouring to save money, they were, nevertheless, mindful that they were tenants, albeit fortunate ones. So to have a home on their own land was beyond their expectations.

Invaluable associates of the Mortimers in the district, Jack and Miriam Henderson, with their two sons Clive and Cameron, were invited to Mirrimbali for Sunday lunch. Accompanying them was their young niece Jess, who had recently arrived as a bounty passenger, with Highland relations, now settled in Melbourne. Life had been tough and cold in the north of Scotland, and Jess, unlike the Mortimer sisters, was loving time with her cousins on their Murray River station. It was never too hot for Jess, and unlike most young ladies of her era, she had insisted on learning to swim. Miriam, her aunt, was somewhat shocked, but Jess didn't care. She just wore drawers and a vest over her corset. Her cousins didn't care either. They admired Jess's courage. She also loved to accompany Clive and Cameron when they worked on the property. Lined up at the back door were her boots, and unlike other ladies who always rode side-saddle, Jess just jumped astride any horse and took off. She loved to gallop around the station, eventually being called Cowgirl Jess by her cousins.

After Sunday luncheon in the dining room at Mirrimbali, the Hendersons and the Mortimers retired to the sitting room to discuss wool trading, seasons and country life. Alexandra and Adelia joined their parents, quietly sewing in the background during the discussion. The MacLeay children raced outside to play, while the older lads arranged Keepings Off with a ball on the grass. Alistair, Duncan and his friend Lachlan took on Clive and Cameron Henderson. Jess helped Jane and Edith clear the dining room and wash the dishes, before racing outside to support her cousins in the match against their hosts. Ensuring numbers were equal, Jess joined her cousins Clive and Cameron in a bid to outplay Alistair, Duncan and Lachlan. She was lithe and athletic, jumping high and on one or two occasions outplaying the lads. Her cousins were not surprised, but Lachlan and Duncan were particularly impressed. Unlike most of the ladies they knew, to say nothing of the Mortimer sisters, Jess was relaxed, uninhibited, and just so much fun. She was certainly different to most of the conservative ladies the boys had met.

Although Lachlan, Duncan's companion, had loved his time at Mirrimbali, he was keen, after several months to see his relatives in Sydney. A horseback journey to the northern capital was considered by the young Scots; others had done it, but since there were still significant unknown dangers en route, a decision was made to return to Melbourne via horse and carriage, from where they could sail north along the east coast. Jess, also, was scheduled to return to her uncle and aunt, so Jack Henderson asked if the Scottish lads might safely chaperone his niece to her Melbourne relations. When they met the teamster, saddlebags were loaded onto the carriage and the boys were seated outside. Jess was to be accommodated within the coach, but to the coachman's astonishment, dressed in her boots and bonnet, Jess requested that she sit outside with the boys. Duncan and Lachlan laughed, assuring the coachman that Jess would be safe and cared for. Jack Henderson also laughed, as he waved them all goodbye.

Clarence's teamster days were coming to an end. Since the Gold Rush, transport had improved significantly. He now had to compete with a company offering carriage transport several times a week between the river settlement and Melbourne.

Watching her brother disappear down the Mirrimbali driveway made it a very sad day for Jane. The children, as well, were heartbroken to see their dearly loved uncle vanish. 'Come back soon, please, Dunks,' they begged. Hugging them all, he promised he would. But the prospect of travel to Sydney, before sailing to California and crossing the American continent to visit Hunter's family, meant that considerable time would elapse before the MacLeays might see their much-loved uncle again.

Chapter Ten

Months passed and life returned to normal after the excitement of Duncan's stay. Knowing no other environment, the children loved their outback life. Lottie played the piano well, and encouraged Cissy's skills, while both created imaginary games in their tree-house cubby. They all helped round up the sheep and assist at shearing time. Often in the morning after Gideon or JimJim milked Buttercup, their dairy cow, the children would carry in the pail, so Edith could scald the milk and prepare it for drinking. Several times the savvy old cow had escaped. Sandy told his siblings to be very wary and always shut the gate firmly. After one occasion, Sandy on horseback, with his sheep dogs, Red and young Rusty, Ringo had died, took ages to separate Buttercup from the sheep and get her back to the house paddock. Another time she got out and wandered down to the river. Without Buttercup, the family would have no milk.

Sandy loved animals, especially kangaroos, wombats and koalas, while Tam, like his father, would never harm any creature, but realised the native fauna were not compatible with cows, sheep, chickens and goats, and lacked his brother's affection for native wildlife.

Nets were set up in the river to snare fish and, occasionally, delectable crayfish. Confident with the process, Sandy regularly checked the submerged traps and carried the day's catch up to the house. As Jane prepared for dinner one evening, there was no sign of Sandy. Tam and his sisters ran outside calling him and looking in the shed and round the property, but to no avail. Finally, Tam whistled and called Rusty, his brother's pet dog, but still there was no sign of his brother or his favourite dog. Familiar with Sandy's propensity for saving injured wildlife and mindful that darkness was falling, Alistair set off in search of his eldest son. He double-checked the shearing shed, and then walked out to JimJim and Gideon's hut, where overnight they guarded the vast flock. Neither had seen Sandy nor Rusty.

So walking back past the mounting yards, Alistair headed down to the river at the forefront of the homestead, but no sign of the pair was there either. He then walked round the bend and downstream, where the current flowed strongly and the nets were set up. The first thing he saw was Rusty whom he called, but the dog refused to respond. Finally, Alistair reached the motionless dog, only to find Sandy, lying prostrate on the ground, still clutching a large stick in his right hand. A few paces behind, lay the day's catch. Horrified, it took his father just seconds to grasp the dreadful reality that a snake had bitten his 12-year-old son.

Instinctively he felt for some sign of life, although the tragic truth was evident. Lifting up the lifeless body of his adored son, he trudged back to the homestead, Rusty by his side. Alistair's mind was in tumult. Darling Jane, Tam and his sisters; how would life go on without their idolised Sandy? This older brother had been their role model; he had taught them so much. Tam, who had been standing on the veranda, came racing down the steps, to help what he perceived to be his wounded brother. Injuries were common occurrences, but death was inconceivable! His father's face told him the news, after which he could barely walk. He continued in some sort of trance, behind his father and Rusty.

Reaching the veranda, Alistair collapsed on a seat, rocking his lifeless son back and forth in inconsolable grief. Tam tiptoed inside and clung to his mother, speechless. Instinctively Jane knew something catastrophic had occurred. She took Tam by the hand and they went out the front door. Unaware, Lottie and Cissy were reading together in the sitting room beside the fire.

All the MacLeay children were conversant with the danger of snakes, namely to never agitate them. They all had experienced scary challenges, and understood one must quietly distance oneself with minimal noise. Sandy had demonstrated this numerous times. However, when dragging in the nets, and facing the water with his back to the scrub, an unseen snake had slithered silently down the sandbank and fatally bitten him. Crying out in agony, Sandy had grabbed a stick, and lashed at the serpent. But the snake had outmanoeuvred his weak and dying prey, slithering into the water. In excruciating agony, the family's beloved son and brother had staggered a couple of steps up the bank, before collapsing dead on the sand. Faithful Rusty, equally shattered, refused to leave his master and remained beside him until Alistair arrived at sunset.

The heartbreak for the MacLeay family was inconceivable. Eventually Alistair carried his lifeless son inside and lay his body in a blanket on a table in the den. Instinct must have communicated the tragedy to Gideon and JimJim who abandoned their watch and called to Edith at the back door. With tears streaming down her face, Edith relayed the heartbreaking news. Gideon put his arms around her as she sobbed uncontrollably. In disbelief, the MacLeays' three loyal helpers gradually absorbed this tragic reality. Edith had wondered if perhaps Gideon and JimJim could row across the river for help but, of course, nothing could be done. JimJim also was weeping. Feeling powerless and grief-stricken, Gideon eventually thought about what Charlie Chester would do in this situation. Taking JimJim's arm, the pair collected some timber and headed into the shed. Darkness had set in, but in candlelight they commenced building a coffin. Then at daybreak, they headed down past the river bend on to the MacLeays' land to a site where they knew Sandy would wish to rest and commenced digging a grave.

Struggling to function, Alistair was overwhelmed when

he discovered what Gideon and JimJim had done. Sandy's body with one or two treasures was placed in the coffin. With Alistair's arm around Jane, and Lottie, Tam and Cissy clinging to their parents, the MacLeay family, with Edith, followed Gideon and JimJim as they carried Sandy to his final resting place. It was a short walk from the homestead. As they stood beside the grave at the river's edge, the blue cloudless sky somehow seemed like a message from their firstborn. I'm with you all. Please keep going for me. Alistair read a passage from the Bible. Supporting her three sobbing children, all of whom were clinging to their mother, Jane somehow survived her adored son's burial. Because Sandy's presence was so dominant in all their lives, accepting his death was heartbreaking. Just for the moment, no one knew how life would go on without him.

Tam and his sisters did not want to go back to school. How could they without Sandy? But their mother was adamant. In times of tragedy, the best thing one could do was endeavour to live as previously, which Sandy would have wanted. '*He will be in your hearts each day.*' Tam, Lottie and Cissy each chose tiny little items of their brother's which they placed in their pockets and took to school, feeling his presence with them. Gideon rowed them upstream to the wharf and for the first few days walked to school with them, after which the trio went by themselves.

Wonderful love and support was given by families from miles around. Everyone shared their excruciating grief. Even people they barely knew wrote loving letters, most delivered to their mailbox at the property entrance, although some flowers and other notes came via the river and were left in containers on the landing. The entire school of St Mary's was in grief. Everyone knew and loved Sandy. He had been such fun, a leader and one of their first pupils. A decision was made to call the entrance room, where the children stored their bags and ate their lunch on wet days, the Sandy MacLeay Room. Jane told the children she always talked to Sandy in the morning, when she confided in him, and that way she did not miss him so much. Lottie said she liked to talk to Sandy before she went to sleep, because then she told him everything that had happened at school, or else, what the animals and plants were doing, according to the season. Lottie thought Sheila Lester was mean, but talking to Sandy helped, because although she knew he agreed, she was sure that Sandy would say, just ignore her and play with other friends. Tam could only talk to Sandy if he felt Sandy could hear him, so like Rusty, he always walked round to Sandy's grave. This was helpful, especially when he wanted to use Sandy's favourite things. However, one day, Tam came home from school very upset, because Miss O'Donnell had told the class that *'Pets can't go to heaven.'* So now Tam didn't want to go there, and he was sure Sandy would leave if Rusty and Red couldn't join him, to say nothing of all his beloved native wildlife. But Jane and Alistair reassured Tam that Miss

O'Donnell was not right. All animals will always be welcome in heaven.

Struggling to overcome their tragic loss, the family received a welcome and unexpected surprise late one Friday evening. Galloping up the Mirrimbali track, they saw a horseman. As they headed down to the yards to greet this unknown rider, it quickly became apparent that their dearly loved 'Dunks' had returned.

Jane and Alistair imagined that by now Duncan would be on his way to America to visit Hunter; but no. The Hendersons had written to their niece advising of Sandy's tragic death, and Jess, having loved her time on the Murray, was in regular correspondence with Duncan in Sydney. Just as the young Scots were preparing to set sail across the Pacific, Duncan received Jess's letter advising of Sandy's tragic death. There was for him only one course of action. Lachlan set sail alone; but not to America – without his special travelling companion, Scotland was his destination.

Dismounting from his horse, Duncan ran to his adored sister and held her in his arms. He was unable to speak. When eventually Jane looked into his eyes, tears were streaming down her brother's face. She had never seen a grown man cry. But innately she understood, this was not just for Sandy. This was grief for a mother he never knew, his dearly loved sister who abandoned him when he was 8, a damaged father who was unable to give love which he, himself, had never received, and finally the overwhelming heartbreak of losing his adored nephew. Jane quietly stroked his shoulder as he clung to her. She was adamant that nothing would be done to stop this outpouring of grief. Years of heartache needed to be expressed.

Eventually the tears ceased, but Duncan could not speak. Jane waited as he unsaddled his horse and collected his bag. Slowly they strolled to the homestead and sat before the fire. Observing from a distance, Edith discreetly set a tea tray on the nearby table, before taking care of the children. Jane shared how leaving him at 8 years of age had broken her heart. She also confided her overwhelming love for Alistair, and that if father had agreed to their marriage, this mutual suffering never would have occurred. It was an emotional and distressing session, but it proved to be cathartic for them both, especially for Duncan. For the first time in his life, he allowed his feelings free reign, and communicated his grief and sorrow to his compassionate sister, who not only understood, but confided her own childhood sorrows. Although it was liberating for them both, it was only step one. Their combined shared heartbreak for Sandy then followed.

Duncan remained at Mirrimbali for several months, again assisting Alistair on the property and spending playtime with his adored nieces and nephew. Nothing could bring back dearly loved Sandy, but support for each other at this tragic time was invaluable. Duncan clearly needed this grieving time as much as they did. Minimal reference was made to his forfeited excursion to America, but they did observe correspondence with Jess.

Opening a letter one evening, Duncan instantly expressed surprise and joy, telling his sister that Jess was coming to stay with her Henderson cousins. Within a few weeks of her arrival, news they had anticipated and hoped for became a reality. Duncan and Jess were to be married. Jane was overjoyed! Not only that Duncan was to marry happy, fun-loving Jess, but also that they would be living nearby.

When Duncan set off with Lachlan a few months earlier, Jane had been devastated. His unexpected arrival had filled a void, present in her life ever since she had eloped. And while his stay with her family had temporarily filled that emptiness, acute sadness had returned with his departure. This, combined with the loss of Sandy, meant Jane's heart ached. So news that her dearly loved brother and Jess now would be permanently in their district was beyond her wildest hopes and dreams.

Duncan negotiated a loan with the local bank, enabling him to purchase land with narrow access to the river a few miles further downstream. It was wooded river country, more suitable for cattle than sheep. Jack and Miriam were thrilled for their cherished niece and to have her nearby was a bonus. In memory of Jess's homeland, the newlyweds named their property Argyll.

Prior to his death, Sandy had been all set to commence

boarding school in Melbourne. St Mary's provided only primary education. As junior school was completed, arrangements were made for the girls to attend a ladies' college while Tam commenced at a boys' boarding school, not too far from his sisters. It was where Sandy had been enrolled. In the city, the MacLeay siblings were now a long way from home which was, of course, a huge adjustment. Jane worried about Tam, who lacked the confidence of his older brother, while the girls would have each other for support. Alistair, however, was less concerned. He hoped friendships with other boys would encourage Tam, and despite the colony still being in its formative years, his children, he believed, had received more opportunities than he had been given as a child.

With their three children now absent from Mirrimbali, except for school holidays, the MacLeays occupied themselves with work on the property and local community life, but it was, of course, not the same, and the absence of their children somehow reinforced the loss of their adored Sandy. Initially they had to be strong to sustain Lottie, Tam and Cissy, but now they grieved in a way which hadn't been possible earlier. Sandy's resting place, walking distance from the homestead, was a comfort. Sharing their joint sorrow intimately with each other, Alistair and Jane gradually became stronger. Duncan and Jess, living just a little further downstream at Argyll, produced three littlies, Campbell,

Maisie and Stuart, in close succession. Just a few miles away, they were a loving focus, particularly for Jane.

Another unexpected visitor arrived in the form of an emancipated convict from Port Arthur. Roddy McDowell, who had been transported from Manchester on the same ship as Gideon, somehow tracked down his old mate. Roddy, it was apparent, had only a short time to live. Mindful of his dire state, the MacLeays did all they could to provide Gideon's friend with comfort and care. He lasted just three weeks before dying. However, what the MacLeays did not know was that Roddy had discovered a valuable nugget on the Ballarat Goldfields, but had never traded his discovery, retaining it as treasure. Combined with Roddy's desire to face death in caring company was his mission to bequeath his Ballarat gold nugget to Gideon. Their mutual homeland, Manchester, held minimal appeal. Since his emancipation, Roddy had managed to support himself, crossing Bass Strait and living a simple life in Melbourne.

Gideon gratefully accepted his gold bequest, but it was to have disastrous consequences, which became apparent with the arrival one night of a despicable thug. Hal Jones had served time with Roddy and Gideon at Port Arthur. Aware of Roddy's good fortune on the goldfields, this contemptible thief was determined the nugget would be his. After spying on Gideon and JimJim, Hal hid himself in the shed. Then hearing the boys return, he suddenly appeared in the dark, confronting Gideon and demanding either Roddy's gold nugget or death.

Shocked and in disbelief, Gideon remained motionless, until Hal, with great force, swung a shovel at his victim. Standing some distance away but watching with vigilance, JimJim hurled himself on Hal just as he raised the spade. Without JimJim's intervention, this thrust most certainly would have been fatal. Gideon's head was spared, but blood seeped from his chest. Several ribs were broken, but thankfully the damage was not worse. Gratitude to JimJim knew no bounds.

Barking dogs alerted Alistair who rushed to the shearers' quarters and instantly helped JimJim restrain Hal Jones with ropes and lock him up. The pair then supported Gideon as he stumbled to the homestead where Jane did her best to ameliorate his wounds and pacify him after this terrifying ordeal.

The next day, Gideon remained in bed at the homestead while JimJim assisted Alistair to transport the villain, restrained and harnessed in their wagon, across the river to the settlement, where Alistair handed him over for internment in the local gaol. A week later Hal Jones was transported to Melbourne.

Stories of bushrangers to the north were common, but thankfully no frightening instances had ever been experienced in their district. It was a terrifying occurrence for everyone at Mirrimbali, but they all were extremely thankful to JimJim, without whom Gideon almost certainly would be dead. Alistair and Jane also were relieved that the children were at boarding school and had not witnessed this heinous crime. As news spread of the incident, settlers in the district became warier and more protective of themselves and their property. Mirrimbali had always been so peaceful.

After Gideon recovered, he asked Jane and Alistair what might be the best way to sell his gold nugget. Other than provision for himself and JimJim, he wished to donate any surplus to the Murray River district, where the best years of his life had been spent. By reason of his injuries, contribution towards building a hospital, which locals recently had proposed, seemed a good idea. Jane and Alistair, mindful of numerous charlatans at the time of the Gold Rush, believed that the best person to oversee the exchange of this nugget would be Hugh Mortimer. The latter's contacts would be reliable and trustworthy.

Alistair wrote to Hugh who kindly agreed. The transaction was not urgent, but in due course, the nugget, transported to Melbourne, was sold and Hugh Mortimer opened a bank account in Gideon's name, where he placed the money. It wasn't a vast sum, but for this emancipated convict, it was more than he had ever dreamed of. Peace of mind and financial security were feelings he had never experienced when growing up in Manchester. He had lived on the streets since he was 10. In addition, Gideon was sure that his old friend Roddy would support this decision of contributing his generous legacy towards a hospital in the local community. Gideon's time at Mirrimbali, while not without challenges, had been fulfilling and satisfying in a way he had never experienced in his youth.

Chapter Eleven

IN CONTRAST TO THE TERRIFYING INCIDENT WITH HAL Jones, another unexpected and very welcome surprise appeared on the horizon. In Philadelphia, Hunter had been eagerly awaiting a visit from his brother Duncan, who never arrived, and so he decided to cross the Pacific Ocean with his family and visit both his siblings.

Enclosed with a letter advising of this forthcoming trip were pictures of Hunter's family, including his only daughter, Jane, named after her aunt. The MacLeays had seen photographs of landscapes, but never had they seen personal pictures such as these. Painted portraits were the customary way they knew of recording images. Excited by this new invention, Hunter had engaged a man to take photographs of his family. The MacLeays and Duncan were fascinated to see their American relatives, especially in light of their forthcoming southern vacation.

Hunter had been very successful. Recently his business partner had travelled across the country to Sacramento on the Transcontinental Railroad and was passionate about this new transit to the West and the opportunities, especially with trade, that it would open up for their country. To that end, Hunter decided to share this innovative experience with his family. Upon arrival in California, they would embark on a steamship across the Pacific Ocean to Sydney. The prospect of travelling on a vessel powered by steam, as opposed to sailing, was another motivation. A successful engineer, Hunter loved experimenting and experiencing new inventions.

Preferring a trip back to Scotland and apprehensive about an expedition involving such time and distance, Jeanie, his wife, was initially less than enthusiastic. Reluctant to accompany her husband, she preferred to remain in Philadelphia with the children. But Hunter had always been a man of spirit and returning to Scotland to see Walter and Gordon at Kirkfeldy held minimal appeal for him, compared to a journey to the southern continent where his younger siblings had settled. He decided that a maid would accompany them, so that the journey would, he hoped, be a rest for his wife. Jeanie appreciated her husband's thoughtful gesture, but since the expedition would involve significant time on board both a train and a ship, Jeanie believed she could manage, and that holiday time together as a family was what would make this voyage special and memorable. Although still tentative, Jeanie acquiesced to Hunter's proposal. Particular educational books were selected which the children were to read during their journey. Luckily, the young Sinclairs shared their father's enthusiasm and so the family set off from the northern hemisphere in autumn, for arrival on the southern continent in late spring. To Hunter's delight, his wife and children loved the transcontinental journey. It reinforced to them the vastness and beauty of America. After a few days absorbing the wonderful sights in San Francisco, the family boarded a steamship for Sydney. To Jeanie's relief, the steamship provided a reasonably smooth voyage with only a few rough days, unlike sailing from Scotland years earlier.

Not only the Sinclair family, but also everyone aboard the *Southern Star* was amazed at the beauty of Sydney Harbour when they sailed through the heads. San Francisco had mesmerised them, but this was of equal splendour. It was a stunning bay with countless inlets meandering in and out of sandy beaches.

After a brief respite in Sydney, Hunter, Jeanie and the children sailed south to Melbourne. More time to explore the beautiful harbour town would have been valued, but for Hunter, the inland destination with his siblings during the southern summer was his first priority. Upon arrival in Melbourne, less established than Sydney, they travelled north to Mirrimbali Station.

Hector, Janie, Jock and Douglas Sinclair were slightly older than their MacLeay cousins. Hector had just finished school and to his parents' delight had been accepted at the University of Pennsylvania, while Janie, Jock and Douglas were 16, 14 and 12 respectively, the same age as Lottie, Tam and Cissy.

Hunter presumed that he would be hiring a carriage to transport his family to the river settlement but, especially since the Gold Rush, the new colony was, like America, advancing in engineering. A railway line had been constructed from Melbourne to the Murray River settlement, near where his siblings Jane, Duncan, and their families, had settled. The train went first to Sandhurst, a gold-mining town, where they stayed overnight. It was very different from Philadelphia and wandering some distance from the town centre, the children observed wombats, kangaroos and emus which, to their surprise, appeared not remotely disturbed by the presence of visitors, although a local boy did advise them that an emu's kick could be unexpected and injurious, if you got too close. En route back to their hotel, Jock, who had wandered off, suddenly called out to his siblings in great excitement. A curious little creature covered in spikes was waddling along the path. Even Hector did not know the name of this extraordinary native animal. It was, they discovered, called an echidna. Taking a pencil and notebook from his pocket, Hector recorded the exact spelling, because he knew that such an unusual name would never be remembered.

Excitement engulfed the entire Sinclair family, especially the children, knowing that tomorrow after this long journey they would meet their New South Wales cousins. A few hours after boarding the train, they peered excitedly out the window as the whistle blew and the locomotive puffed into Echuca Station. Carriages awaited the arrival of passengers. Hunter approached a young man, enquiring whether he might be able to transport them to Mirrimbali Station. The local lad replied yes; he had visited that river run previously. A bridge soon was to be built across the Murray, connecting the State of Victoria to New South Wales on the northern side, but presently the only possible transit was via a punt.

With luggage on board the carriage, Jane's brother Hunter and his family set off on the final stage of this exciting and prolonged journey. After crossing the river and travelling along a dusty track, they approached Mirrimbali. In contrast to gum trees everywhere, the American visitors admired the stately oaks lining the long driveway. This outback countryside was so different from their homeland. That English oaks had survived here was a miracle.

As their carriage came up the driveway, Alistair, Jane, Lottie, Tam and Cissy were waiting on the front veranda to greet their American cousins. As when Duncan had arrived, Jane greeted her brother Hunter with a long and profound embrace. The prospect of ever seeing any of her family again after her elopement had been remote.

Although the cousins had never met, there was instant loving interaction between them all. And after a brief visit inside the homestead, the children raced outside, around the property and down to the river to take in the Murray's spectacular views.

Alistair instinctively knew that, as with Duncan, Jane would value time with her brother, whom she had not seen for 20 years and who had travelled halfway across the world. So he escorted Jeanie into the homestead, to her bedroom and then round the house. Gideon and JimJim carried in the trunks, while Edith prepared tea and cakes for the overseas visitors.

Hunter valued this quiet interlude with Jane. First and foremost was his need to divulge to her his enduring guilt, brought about by his role in thwarting her initial elopement with Alistair. He had always regretted not challenging his father. But now, he was so happy that she and Alistair had fled Kirkfeldy for a life together in this new southern land. As they hugged, Jane shed tears; there were so many memories. But as with Duncan, it felt cathartic, never needing to be referred to again. And as a parent, she understood how Hunter, a naïve young man, had no choice but to obey his father. After their emotional session, Hunter headed straight to his brother-in-law, sharing his regrets regarding their first elopement. To Alistair, however, it was past history and not an issue. But when Hunter went to sleep that night, he was relieved at how much more peaceful he felt, by reason of admitting his mistake and apologising.

The seven young cousins were on a high, with so much excitement! Just when it seemed that nothing more exhilarating could occur, a cart drove up with Duncan, Jess and their trio. The MacLeays raced to meet their little cousins and introduce to them the exciting older Americans. Joy among Jane and her brothers Hunter and Duncan, was equal to that of the younger generation. Duncan and Jess's little trio, Campbell, Maisie and Stuart, living on their remote farm and unused to such liveliness, were initially somewhat shy and overcome. But Hector, Janie, Jock and Douglas Sinclair took them into their arms. Campbell and Maisie had some comprehension of their connection, but it was beyond 4-year-old Stuart. He had trouble keeping up, so Hector and Janie, as her siblings called her, took turns to carry him. In no time, he was loving the attention, especially riding on Hector's shoulders, while the older cousins filial connection was instantly innate. They all adored each other. Gideon and JimJim, as well as Edith, observed the scene with fascination.

Duncan and Jess would love to have stayed longer, but at the end of a memorable day the approaching dusk signalled it was time to climb into their cart. After all, tomorrow they would be together again. Jane had planned a large Sunday roast, to be shared with her two brothers and their families. Never, when she fled Scotland, did she conceive that Hunter and Duncan both would travel vast distances to find her in New South Wales. The value she placed on their love, and the respective journeys they had undertaken to find her, was priceless.

Without the adults even realising it, Lottie, Tam and Cissy had earlier taken Hector, Janie, Jock and Douglas beyond the river bend to Sandy's grave. Although a tragic site, it was overwhelmed with love. The American Sinclairs had never met Sandy, but they felt as if they knew him. The siblings' enduring devotion to their brother, as well as stories they had heard, meant Sandy's presence was with them all, as they held hands, hugged and led by Hector, said a little prayer. With Sandy in their hearts, they then wandered further round to a favourite sandbank where Lottie, Tam and Cissy reminisced about their dearly loved brother. Lots of fun, tree climbing and other games were enjoyed, which was just what Sandy would have wanted.

After Duncan, Jess and their three little children departed, Hide and Seek was enjoyed, before it was time to return to the homestead. Dinner was followed by ablutions and donning night attire, after which the cousins settled into beds along the rear, covered-in veranda. It was a warm summer evening, still light, without a breath of wind. Mindful of winter now at home, the American cousins loved this warm temperature, as well as viewing the southern hemisphere stars, which could be seen while lying in their beds. Equally fascinating were the cries of unfamiliar wildlife.

After a quiet spell listening to night sounds, Hector, from his bed in the middle, commenced recounting tales about Philadelphia, the Liberty Bell and American history. He was a gifted young man, with a photographic memory. Although Cissy was exhausted after the day's activities, she was totally engrossed with Hector's narratives, and nothing would induce her to sleep. The voyage of the *Mayflower* in 1620 was fascinating, more than 150 years before any settlement in Australia. Then the War of Independence was explained. The MacLeay children knew some history about their homeland and Europe, but knowledge of America was minimal.

Hector was fascinating. For settlers who had headed west across an unknown continent, courage and fortitude had been required, but it had all contributed to what was now a free and democratic nation. Hector's last recollections were very powerful, because they involved incidents actually witnessed by him. As a little boy, he observed life when the Civil War erupted between the North and South of the country. Some aggressive conflicts had taken place in Philadelphia between groups passionate about their respective causes. During the Gettysburg campaign, their neighbour's son had been killed and Hector relayed that many people were frightened that the battle might spread to their city. The passion with which Hector described these events had the children totally mesmerised. All the MacLeay cousins dreamed of visiting America one day.

On following nights, Hector entertained his cousins with other colourful stories about their life in Philadelphia as well as poetry recitals. When quite young, Hunter had offered his eldest son a tempting reward if he could memorise some poems of their famous Scottish bard, Robbie Burns. Keen for this remuneration, Hector had acquiesced to his father's request. As well as memorising Burns' poems, he recited them in the engaging Scottish accent, making his narrations all the more intriguing. The MacLeay children knew a few sonnets, but nothing in the class of Hector. Whenever his recitals ended, Cissy always begged for more, but Hector's response was invariably a firm *'No! That's enough for tonight.'*

Totally captivated by her cousin, and curious about everything, Cissy had one precise query. What was a university? Hector explained it was an institution where extra learning was acquired after school. When she was puzzled why more knowledge would be needed, Hector assured Cissy that ladies rarely attended, generally just men. To qualify as a doctor, engineer or lawyer, additional knowledge and specific skills were required. Cissy did not think Tam would ever be interested.

The next day, Duncan and Jess arrived well before lunch, so there was ample time for the cousins to again play some wonderful games together. Keepings Off, Hide and Seek, to say nothing of the Big Bad Wolf, played of course by Hector, were just some of their activities. Campbell and Maisie especially adored running for their lives as the Big Bad Wolf howled and charged after them. It was hard to know who enjoyed it more, the active cousins or their observing parents. Alistair and Jane, with her brothers Hunter and Duncan and their wives, particularly valued this special time for their children to be together. How foolish their father had been to deprive himself of such joy.

After a delicious Sunday lunch, preceded by Robbie Burns'

'Grace', *'Some hae meat but canna eat,'* the children were all set to race outside again, when Jeanie seated herself at the piano and commenced playing. She was a gifted musician. Her talent was such, and the music so superb, that no one even considered leaving the room. Familiar with the songs, her three children, Janie, Jock and Douglas, sang and danced around the piano, while talented Hector accompanied her on his banjo. The rest of the family were mesmerised. The MacLeays were familiar mostly with Classical and Scottish music but Jeanie's tunes were wonderful, like nothing they had ever heard before. Unable to sit still, Jess jumped up, grabbed Jane's arm and the two commenced dancing, joined immediately by Alistair, Hunter and Duncan. Soon all the children participated, dancing and singing to this amazing music.

The tunes that captured them were Stephen Foster's classic songs. Although unknown to the MacLeays, Hunter said Foster's compositions were so popular that he was known as the father of American music. In no time, the children were singing and dancing while constantly begging Aunt Jeanie to play them again. 'Camptown Races', 'Oh Susanna', 'The Old Folks at Home', 'Beautiful Dreamer' and 'Jeanie with the Light Brown Hair' soon became favourites. When eventually the excitement died down, Hunter produced a map showing his nieces and nephews where various places they sang about were located. Pennsylvania, Alabama, Kentucky and other states. America looked so exciting that the entire Mirrimbali household were all very keen to visit their cousins one day. As it had to Jeanie, a steamship appealed to Jane much more than the *Esperance* on which they had sailed 20 years ago.

After a lifetime of winter Christmases, Hunter's family enjoyed an excessively hot 25th of December. The traditional roast turkey and ham were served, followed by plum pudding, but instead of being surrounded by snow, sliding on ice and throwing snowballs, the American cousins spent Christmas afternoon swimming at the sandbank. A rope had been hung from a wide eucalypt branch extending out over the water. It was deemed too dangerous for the Philadelphia clan, who were not sufficiently confident swimmers, but to their wonderment, Tam, Lottie and Cissy swung out over the water numerous times, before bouncing into the river and swimming back to the sandbank. Their cousins were fascinated.

The day after Christmas, Hunter announced to his children that in two more days they must leave; it was time for the Sinclairs to return to Philadelphia. Loving the river and watching passing paddle steamers as they waved and acknowledged the children with friendly whistles, Hector asked if the family might travel up the river by boat, and then journey overland to Sydney before sailing across the Pacific to their homeland. Hunter acknowledged that he, also, would love to do that, but while paddle steamers sailed to Albury, the overland journey north would be far too long and tiresome. Unlike in America, there was no direct train line. And so it was that they returned the same way they had arrived.

Early on the last morning, Duncan and Jess came to Mirrimbali with their family to join in the farewell. Hunter's siblings were so grateful to him for making this extraordinary expedition, enabling the next generation to meet. They hugged each other as if they never would let go, but as always, life must go on. Mirrimbali suddenly seemed very dull after their departure; something definitely was missing. But at least now, when they corresponded, the American family could picture the Australian MacLeays and Sinclairs, identifying firsthand with life on the Murray River. And when incidents were shared, they comprehended exactly which cousin was involved. Hunter's siblings and their families hoped that one day they might visit Philadelphia, but such a journey, of course, would be a long way off.

Chapter Twelve

TIME PASSED RAPIDLY AND WITHIN THREE YEARS BOTH Lottie and Tam had left school. Missing bush life, Tam had no desire for further study. Mindful that his parents were still tenants, Tam was desperate to assist them acquire more land. Hugh Mortimer had been generous and appreciative of his father's years of hard work, but Tam wanted independence. Oakbank, the MacLeays' river allotment where the Manager's Cottage had been built, was the extent of their property.

Within two years, news arrived that Henry Mortimer had died and the Yorkshire mill had been sold. His brother Hugh, now retired from his Melbourne practice and financially independent, decided that the time had come to sell Mirrimbali. The MacLeays could not afford to buy the station, but an agreement was reached whereby an allotment adjoining their land was sold to them. Tam was very pleased, as in addition to cattle, he wished to plant crops, and access to the river in drought times would assist this. Passionate about the land and especially its river frontage, Tam had no interest in city or township life. He valued his boarding school education, but there was only one place for him to live and work, in the bush.

Grace Miller, a lovely girl from the local township, crossed his path. They fell in love and were swiftly married. Grace's father tragically had been killed when she was only 7, so life had been very difficult for her mother and siblings. But, as often happens in these situations, Grace benefitted from her challenging childhood. She had sound values and was very compassionate. For Tam, life with Grace at Oakbank resembled the loving atmosphere of his childhood home. Good seasons occurred for their first few years, but then a harsh drought set in and for Tam and his family, life was very stressful. As no rain came, and with insufficient feed, he was forced to sell stock and towards the end, almost gave away many of his cattle, because he couldn't bear to watch them suffer and die.

Ever since he was a young boy, Tam had keenly observed the various seasons, hot, arid summers and cold winters. His main source of frustration was excessive flooding which occurred during some winters. When this happened, water flowed across the vast native forest opposite Oakbank. For miles along the Murray, where banks were low, masses of floodwater spread across sizeable stretches of land. Why couldn't channels be built leading to dams to store this water? Every summer and certainly during the prolonged drought which commenced in the late 1870s, so many desperate farmers were without water. Stock had to be sold before they died and innumerable families were forced off the land and left penniless.

Tam, of course, did not have the resources to activate his ideas, but he was desperate for something to be done. Letters to both the local newspaper and *The Melbourne Argus* were written, expressing his hope of developing some form of water storage – dams, canals or whatever could be constructed. A boarding school friend, Roger, recounted wonderful times during his childhood, when he had travelled along the extensive canal system in England. Tam understood those waterways were created as a means of transport. But nevertheless, could not something like that be built in this country? Sizeable storage dams? Anything, somehow to save water during floods. Tam never gave up hope. Eventually, to his relief and satisfaction, a weir was constructed near Nagambie and another irrigation project was undertaken further downstream at Mildura. For Tam at Oakbank, nothing changed overnight, but at least some action was being taken. As he worked hard and battled through these years of harsh drought, Grace gave birth to two sons and a daughter, Richard, Robert and Rose.

Mirrimbali Station had been sold to Angus Scott, the son of a wealthy property owner from the Blue Mountains. Within a short time of Angus' acquisition, he fell in love with Lottie and requested her hand in marriage. Alistair and Jane acquiesced, delighted to have two of their children nearby. In quick succession, Lottie gave birth to two sons, David and

William. For Alistair and Jane, it was a joyous time. They now derived great pleasure from five little grandchildren: Lottie's two Scott boys and Tam's three MacLeays. The respective cousins, living in close proximity, loved their time together, but there was no question that the lifestyle of Angus and Lottie's children was considerably different to that of Tam and Grace's. Angus was a wealthy landowner, whereas Tam and Grace, having struggled through the drought, were now living very frugally. Cissy finished school and also came home, so that all three MacLeay siblings were near their parents.

With Tam managing Oakbank, and his sister Lottie now living with Angus and their sons on Mirrimbali, Alistair and Jane purchased a home with a lovely garden in the riverside town. Much as they loved the river, Tam was adamant that wherever his parents settled, it must be a significant distance from both the Murray and the Campaspe Rivers, because of winter floods.

Through a Sydney friend, Angus had managed to sell a sizeable property his father owned on the Darling River and to his great satisfaction, the family's long-serving and experienced station manager agreed to relocate south to Mirrimbali. Frequently Angus travelled to Sydney and to his other station west of the Blue Mountains to ensure efficient management. During Angus' absence, Jane and Alistair stayed on the property with Lottie. Thanks to the construction of a bridge across the Murray, it was now much easier to visit Lottie at Mirrimbali than it had been in the days of the punt. Jane and Alistair had been invaluable to their eldest daughter during her pregnancy with David and then 18 months later, when she gave birth to William.

Next door on Oakbank, Tam and Grace also benefitted from Alistair and Jane's help, while Cissy's return to the district was welcomed by both her siblings, especially Lottie. A keen artist, Cissy quickly settled into her parents' new Echuca home, where she commenced painting, producing some beautiful river landscapes, as well as spectacular renditions of paddle steamers.

Suddenly, out of the blue, a handsome young Irishman, Ned Connell, travelling through the outback and temporarily working in the district, met Cissy and began courting her. They instantly fell in love. He inundated her with exciting outings and his constant presence. Cissy adored him, but her parents were more circumspect. Something about Ned was not quite right, but Cissy, young and naïve, saw only his charm. The pair had a wonderful time together, although Alistair frequently asked Tam to keep an eye on his beautiful younger sister. Eventually, to Cissy's delight, Ned asked for her hand in marriage. She was ecstatic, but Ned explained that first he needed temporarily to return to Sydney. Cissy lovingly farewelled him, while she waited in anticipation for their special reunion. However, time passed, and Ned did not return, nor was any word ever received from him. Alistair, Jane and Tam were not surprised, but Cissy was heartbroken.

Every day she excitedly checked their letterbox, hoping in vain for news of Ned.

A delightful older doctor, John Wallace from Melbourne, came to stay with friends for a picnic race meeting and ball. He too fell in love with Cissy. But as he was eight years older, she could not consider him. She was still completely obsessed with Ned Connell. Eventually, through a Sydney cousin, Jess discovered that Ned Connell had married a young girl from the Emerald Isle, and they had sailed to America. Cissy was devastated, and although she tried not to let the news affect her, she became ill and languished.

After some months at home convalescing, Cissy visited Melbourne, where she re-met Dr John Wallace. It was impossible for her to respond to him after the dashing and exciting Irishman, but John was patient. While in Melbourne, he took her to the theatre and music halls. He was a cultured, kind man. Gradually Cissy felt at ease and at home with him, but she could not recreate the passion of her former suitor. She returned to Mirrimbali. John wrote regularly and visited the district once more. Eventually Cissy realised how easily John fitted into her environment and how well he related to her family and friends. Reluctantly, she admitted to herself that while even the mention of Ned Connell's name, let alone his presence, had made every fibre in her being ignite, it was a friendship of highs and lows, inconstancy and unreliability. The stability, dependability and genuine worth of John was the reverse. Finally, to the great joy of all her family, Cissy married John Wallace. She adjusted well to life in Melbourne where John had his medical practice, and for Jane and Alistair it was a welcoming and pleasurable place to stay.

American news from Hunter, Jeanie and their children arrived intermittently by mail. They all seemed to be well. Jock had followed his brother Hector to the University of Pennsylvania and both had graduated, the former as a doctor and the latter as a lawyer. Douglas, taking after his mother, remained true to his passion for music. Janie had married a fine young man and was now living in New York. Duncan and Jess's son Campbell, who as a young lad had been captivated by his American cousins, set off across the Pacific Ocean determined to visit his Sinclair cousins and try his luck in the USA. His parents were apprehensive, but realised that holding him back would achieve nothing. His mother Jess, particularly, hoped that he would return to his homeland before too long.

Chapter Thirteen

Jane and Alistair were enjoying life in the local township and contributing to community activities when suddenly, without warning, another terrible tragedy struck their family. Lottie's two young sons were at boarding school in Melbourne when she again became pregnant. All was well until, while giving birth on their property to her third child, a daughter, she tragically died. The heartbreak was inconceivable, but naturally the MacLeays were on hand to support Angus, his sons and new baby, Sylvie.

Angus' reaction to his loss, however, brought about even more grief. Life on Mirrimbali without his adored Lottie was to him inconceivable and so in great pain and with undue haste, he walked off his property, placed it on the market and settled on his family's sheep station, Milingil, 400 miles north. David and William were taken out of their Melbourne boarding school and a governess was engaged for them, while young Nurse Smith was appointed to care for Sylvie. Angus' grief was not in question, but his solution to this tragic loss was. Many people in the district were shocked, not just by Lottie's death, but also by her husband's response to it.

In addition to losing Lottie, the MacLeays now would rarely see their grandchildren and would have minimal influence in their lives. Duncan, assisted by his wife Jess, endeavoured to support his dear sister Jane, as she and Alistair tried to cope with this second tragedy. Closing the door on his past seemed to be the only way Angus could cope.

For Jane and Alistair, their grief was compounded. Not only had they lost Sandy and Lottie, but now their beautiful grandchildren David, William and baby Sylvie were 400 miles away. For Jane this felt like history repeating itself. She and her brothers had lost their mother when very young and now her grandchildren were experiencing the same heartbreak. But why could Angus not see that his children were entitled to consideration? What was best for everyone mattered, not just what was right for him. That Angus was far from well was apparent, but the consequences of his behaviour were extremely distressing, particularly for his motherless children. Shattered though the MacLeays were, they nevertheless endeavoured to remain compassionate and supportive of Angus during his sudden, dramatic and erratic behaviour after Lottie's tragic death.

Cissy was especially heartbroken. Not only had she lost her older sister and role model, but she adored David and William and wanted to help them and their little baby sister.

But now, as they were located 160 miles west of Sydney, contact was impossible. However, Jane's advice to all her family was sound. Although the MacLeays were grieving and very upset at the choice made by Angus, there was nothing they could do. Loving patience was their only recourse.

Cissy wrote several times to her brother-in-law, enquiring if she could help with the children in any way, but nothing was forthcoming. Eventually, 18 months later, a letter arrived inviting Cissy and John to stay at Milingil Station, west of the Blue Mountains, for a picnic race meeting and a ball. In addition, Angus advised that he had met and married Lady Audrey Parker, who was visiting from England. A home in Sydney with beautiful views across the harbour had also been purchased. Apparently outback life held minimum appeal for Lady Audrey, who chose to dwell principally at their bayside residence. However, in order to maintain his various stations, significant time in the country was required by Angus.

Cissy wrote back thanking Angus and advising that she and John would be delighted to attend. Her main purpose, naturally, was to see the children about whom she had been so worried. As anticipated, she had little in common with Lady Audrey or the other house guests, but time with her nephews and newborn niece was wonderful, to say nothing of David and William's response to their dearly loved uncle and aunt. Baby Sylvie, fortunately, seemed to be flourishing under Nurse Smith's care. Now teenagers, Lottie's boys were handsome young men, but unsurprisingly, both lacked confidence. Their time at Milingil Station since their mother's death had clearly been very difficult. With their father mostly absent, love and support at this tragic grieving time came only from a governess, Nurse Smith, and a young maid, who cooked and cleaned. Since Lottie's death, there clearly had been very little emotional support from their father.

Cissy read to them each night, recited verses, played the piano and went for walks around the property with her nephews. John joined in too. Of course, they were not her children and it was not her business, but after observing life on Milingil Station, towards the end of her stay Cissy decided to approach Angus with a couple of suggestions. Whatever course he chose, was naturally his prerogative. With tact and gentleness, Cissy queried how Angus might feel about returning the boys to boarding school in Melbourne, rather than Sydney as planned. With no children of their own to care for, Cissy and John would do all they could to support David and William. This would include weekends with their uncle, aunt and occasionally their grandparents. Angus thanked Cissy, but responded that his sons would commence at a Sydney boarding school in the new year.

Lottie had provided a perfect balance in Angus' life and it seemed that subconsciously he blamed his last child for her death. Cissy understood that his English bride was beautiful, but she was cold, calculating and had very little interest in Angus' children. Sylvie's nurse was the children's only constant presence. Lady Audrey led a high profile life. All her movements were recorded in the society pages of the Sydney newspapers. She was the reverse of Lottie. The children remained at Milingil Station, rarely seeing their father or stepmother. Cissy was fond of Angus, but she found it difficult to penetrate the hard shell which he appeared to have formed as a defence against the pain of Lottie's death. That he could not find solace and comfort by supporting his children, who were young, innocent and also hurting badly, was beyond Cissy's comprehension.

Moving to a new school in Sydney was a sizeable adjustment for David and William, but fortunately the brothers were close and supported each other. According to reports, they seemed to have settled in well, however, both shared ongoing grief for their mother and a mutual antipathy towards Lady Audrey. They enthusiastically accepted an invitation to stay with Aunt Cissy in Melbourne and visit their grandparents during the next school holidays.

After returning to their Melbourne home, next door to John's medical practice, Cissy gradually came to accept that she was unlikely to have children. She had suffered a very distressing miscarriage and in the years since had been unable to conceive. Her thoughtful and caring husband was a special treasure, but their inability to have a family was a source of grief. On the positive side, however, when Cissy looked at life and the tragedies she had witnessed among her family and friends, she realised she was very blessed. Her father, Alistair, had often recounted how his mother's two sisters had died in childbirth.

After visiting her parents on the Murray River, it was clear to Cissy that the trauma of Lottie's death and its consequences, compounded by Angus' behaviour, had taken a sizeable toll on her parents, but particularly on Jane. Involved in community activities, they were enjoying life in the Echuca township, while regular contact with Tam's family at Oakbank was, of course, a special bonus. Even though his strength and energy had diminished, it was clear that Alistair missed life on the land, but it was her mother's appearance that worried Cissy. At the time of Sandy's death, Jane had shown unbelievable courage and fortitude, but now she was overwhelmed by Lottie's tragic passing. Her health clearly had been affected. She was extremely thin and seemed to have very limited energy. Wondering if John, perhaps, could help restore her mother's health, Cissy brought her parents to their Elwood home with its adjoining medical practice. After John's comprehensive examination of his mother-in-law, he confided to Cissy that he was not hopeful of her recovery. Sadly, Jane was terminally ill.

There would be no return to the Murray River. After six weeks at Elwood, Jane quietly passed away with dearly loved Alistair and Cissy by her side. She confided that she held no regrets and was so very grateful to have enjoyed a wonderful life with dearest Alistair, her beautiful children and her grandchildren in this southern continent. A fine role model,

Jane never had indulged in self-pity and her love was always unconditional.

Her family knew Jane would like to have been laid to rest near darling Sandy, but the practicalities of transporting her there were not viable. Instead, she was buried in a nearby cemetery, with provision for Alistair to ultimately join her. Tam and Grace with their children, as well as her dear brother Duncan with Jess and their family, travelled to Melbourne for her funeral service. Cam Sinclair, Duncan's eldest son, had returned from America and was now in Sydney, to his parents' great relief. They couldn't wait to see him again at Argyll, although Duncan and Jess believed that Stuart would be the one to manage the property long term, which proved to be correct. An adventurous spirit, Cam next travelled to the West, where he settled in Perth, marrying a local girl.

Although Jane's departure left a huge vacuum in all their lives, the wonderful example of how she had lived, sustained her family. Even her little grandchildren often quoted *'Granny Jane's'* wise words, or recounted an inspiring action she had taken. Tam arranged the sale of his parents' Echuca home. Life there without darling Jane was not possible for Alistair. In agreement with his children, a decision was made that he would share his time with both their families. Initially he lived mainly at Elwood with Cissy and John. It was just a short walk to the beach, which he loved. Naturally, frequent train trips to the Murray continued, enabling him to spend time at Oakbank, observing the innovative work Tam was carrying out. Alistair missed his darling Jane, but like her, he was unselfish and appreciated his children's kind support.

Throughout all this trauma, Tam and his wife Grace were working hard on their Oakbank property with their three children, Richard, Robert and Rose. As it had been during Tam's childhood, the homestead was a loving environment. Everyone was welcome.

After the sale of Mirrimbali, Gideon moved to the river township. He had continued working with the MacLeays for many years, but his strength had never been the same after Hal Jones bashed him, while JimJim sadly had died, but with Gideon by his side it was a peaceful end. A young boy who had grown up next to Grace's family in the township now worked at Oakbank with Tam. He loved life on the land and valued all that he was learning.

Chapter Fourteen

SHORTLY AFTER JANE'S DEATH, A LETTER ARRIVED FROM Angus Scott to say that he had agreed to sail to England with Lady Audrey, and to that end, he wondered if Cissy might be able to care for Sylvie during their absence, approximately 10 months, as well as his sons, David and William, during the holidays. Nurse Smith would accompany his little daughter to Melbourne. Now 5, Sylvie was due to commence school in the new year. David and William would arrive by train at the end of term. Of course, Cissy not only acquiesced, but replied that she would be delighted to mind her little niece and two nephews. John was in agreement, but appreciating that it was a sizeable responsibility for his wife, he arranged through an assistant at his practice to employ a young girl nearby, for help during this time. Although Angus would be absent for months, it did seem that finally he was giving his children's needs some consideration. How different were the lives of the entire Scott family since the death of Lottie and the arrival of Lady Audrey?

Cissy and John's home, next to the medical practice, was

not on the scale of the Scotts' home, but David, William and Sylvie were very happy there. When Grandy stayed, it was a bit crowded, but the boys made room for their grandfather in the spare bedroom, with the second brother sleeping in the sitting room. Sylvie slept in her aunt and uncle's room. At Elwood, the boys loved racing down to the beach where they enjoyed fun on the sand, building castles and searching for shells. Their only regret was how much colder the water was than in Sydney. Sylvie, accompanied by Nurse Smith, arrived first, followed by her brothers three weeks later. A little primary school was within walking distance and opposite a park. Sylvie was enrolled and all set to commence there in the New Year, during her father's overseas absence. Having never known her mother, Sylvie adored her uncle and aunt, and in turn, brought special love and joy into their home. David and William also loved Cissy and John and especially valued time they could now spend with their little sister, whom they had seen rarely.

Christmas at Elwood was very happy, and just before New Year's Day, bags were packed, and they caught the train up to the Murray where, with much joy, they stayed at Uncle Tam and Aunty Grace's farm, Oakbank. It was a bit crowded, but no one cared. For Alistair, time with his children and grandchildren was invaluable. His thoughts, nevertheless, were often with darling Jane and their two absent offspring, Sandy and Lottie. To reduce numbers, Alistair offered to go across to Argyll and stay with his brother-in-law Duncan and Jess. It was just a few miles away by horse and cart, not too long a journey. But Grace and Tam were adamant that he must remain. As well as Alistair enjoying this special interaction with his grandchildren, he added an invaluable dimension to all their lives. Everyone would remember this holiday!

Since the death of their mother, the Scott children had not experienced any family holidays at Easter or Christmas like those of their childhood. Lady Audrey was totally occupied attending social functions in Sydney, so the children were required to entertain themselves. Staff minded them, cooking and cleaning, but no emotional support or interactive engagement was offered by their stepmother, while their father spent significant time overseeing management of his Milingil station.

So for David, William and Sylvie, holidays with the MacLeay cousins on their Murray River farm was wonderful. The older brothers reminisced about childhood memories on Mirrimbali, mother teaching them to ride, and learning to swim in the river. Since commencing boarding school in Sydney, their father's property west of the Blue Mountains was rarely visited. When not at school, time was spent at their Sydney harbourside home.

In contrast, Tam's children, Richard, Robert and Rose MacLeay, led a very simple life on Oakbank, with few indulgences. Respective chores on the property and round the house were done by them as a normal routine. On arrival, the Scott cousins were enthusiastically welcomed, to say nothing of Aunt Cissy and Uncle John. Oakbank was basic, with minimal furnishings, but it was a relaxed and loving home. Five extras in the house and their grandfather meant lots of work for Grace. But unlike some households, here, from the moment you walked through the front door, you knew you were in a loving and caring environment. Grace never fussed. Somehow, everything just fell into place and if it didn't, then it wasn't a major issue. Daily life flowed smoothly, although Cissy's thoughtful assistance, with cooking, cleaning and extra chores, certainly was valued.

Unlike time David and William had spent on their father's station at Milingil mostly horse riding, life at Oakbank was tedious and hard work, to say the least. Young Richard and Robert MacLeay were working on a project for their father, to clear the property of a noxious weed with sharp prickles which had spread extensively. Initially, the Scott brothers were appalled at having to undertake such labour, especially in excessive heat. But as they rolled up their sleeves and joined their cousins, digging into the dry soil to extract masses of this pestilential sward, they gradually felt a sense of satisfaction. A mammoth pile had been amassed, which ultimately would be burnt. It grew bigger and bigger as more weeds were gathered and hurled onto the stack. Many hands make light work, but much more, still, was to be done.

The four boys slaved diligently for two weeks. Although it was a colossal undertaking, the end proved to be an extraordinary achievement. Uncle Tam was overjoyed. Never could he have cleared his property of this noxious weed. It would have continued to spread, causing significant damage. Without the diligent and continuous hard work of these four young men, the property would have been profoundly impacted. Tam could not have afforded to pay workers, and even if he had borrowed money, the likelihood of finding locals willing to undertake this unappealing task, was remote.

In contrast to their initial reaction, David and William felt a huge sense of satisfaction at what they, with their cousins, had achieved for Uncle Tam. In turn, the latter's gratitude to his sons and nephews knew no bounds. The Scott brothers, knowing nothing else, had always taken their father's resources for granted. But living at Oakbank and being mindful of not wasting water or causing any expensive outlay was a very real awakening for the boys. Uncle Tam's minimal resources exposed a very different reality to life as the Scott brothers knew it.

Uncle John had stayed for just a week, before returning to maintain his busy Elwood practice. Two weeks later, observing the Scott trio happy and relaxed at Oakbank, Cissy asked whether Grace could manage the cousins while she caught the train home briefly, to support her husband. Both Tam and Grace were completely relaxed with the status quo. Tam, particularly, felt incredibly appreciative of his nephews' contribution.

Although it was only a brief spell before Cissy returned, she gradually became aware of changes in both David and Will. A subtle but quiet confidence, in stark contrast to the underlying grief which both boys had manifested since their mother's death, was slowly emerging. Although they were restrained, the changes were apparent to loving eyes. In this safe and caring household, shyness and reserve seemed to have retreated, being replaced by positivity and self-esteem. It was a heartening transformation. Usually shy and lacking in confidence the brothers could be overheard laughing after playing harmless tricks on their naïve cousins. Engaging each day with Richard and Robert as they helped around the farm, David and William had subconsciously realised that this was the best holiday they had ever had. There was, of course, time to play, and swim at the sandbank, but never for one minute, regardless of what they were doing, had they been bored. Most days involved hard work, often tedious and dull, but lots of things about life on the land were learned, skills which they had never understood during their childhood. Their parents, especially Mother, had provided love and life's tangibles, but it was not like staying with Uncle Tam and Aunty Grace.

Sylvie had never known her mother and spent minimal time with her father, so she was not on the same page as her older brothers. Fortunately, the boys were close, just 18 months apart. Adjusting to life's challenges, they had always supported each other. Outwardly, they seemed fine, but inwardly, both lacked confidence. So observing an increase in their self-assurance during this stay at Oakbank was, to their aunt Cissy, very pleasing. Humour and lightheartedness were elements in their changed attitudes. Whether they worked or played, laughter among the cousins could be heard regularly. This definitely was a new perspective.

One morning, looking out the window, Cissy observed Tam's three, Richard, Robert and Rose, watching in fascination as William performed acrobatics across the grass. Encouraged by David, he did cartwheels, somersaults, backflips and then walked on his hands. The MacLeay cousins clapped and cheered at this incredible performance. Only once before had Cissy ever seen William demonstrate these skills. Despite his amazing ability, William usually was too shy ever to perform in front of anyone. Only with reluctance would he ever enact these amazing feats. But she hoped this was another sign of increased confidence and self-esteem. Grace, also, came out to watch, and to Cissy's delight, William was not deterred. While David was talented academically, Will was a gifted athlete.

For the Scott brothers, holidaying at Oakbank with their relations became an insightful experience. Although it was not intended, their summer holiday created an overwhelming and lasting impact. It was positive and life-changing. Unspoken, it proved to be an innate realisation, which subconsciously affected them. Living as the MacLeays lived and staying close to them was how David and William wished to live. Tam and Grace were not conscious of their influence. This was just normal life, how they existed.

Angus Scott's values had dominated his sons' childhood. Wealth was a foremost feature and it was openly demonstrated that the important principles in life pertained to appearance. How people presented themselves and what they possessed, was what mattered. Although not verbally expressed, these values were visibly confirmed by Lady Audrey and their father. At Oakbank, principles were the reverse. There was no question in David and William's mind, after experiencing this holiday, as to how they wished to live. Inner peace far exceeded outward appearances.

Clearly life for Uncle Tam, Aunt Grace and their children had been tough. Hopefully they would survive the current drought; they had done so before. The Oakbank MacLeays may not have had money, but they had things that money cannot buy. It was a house full of love and unconditional support. It was relaxed with no strict rules, yet the Scott brothers had observed their three cousins being strongly disciplined. Fairly and firmly corrected, but not meanly as one sometimes witnessed at boarding school. At Oakbank everyone felt safe, secure and at peace.

For David and Will, it was refreshing to be once again in the river-land of their childhood. Although nominally they had led more privileged lives, attending exclusive boarding schools and living in a luxurious home with superb views across Sydney Harbour, ever since the death of their mother they had experienced minimal love and support. Oakbank was another world. Life was simple, but it was a loving home full of kindness and affection. Richard and Robert attended Echuca Collegiate School while Rose was a pupil at the State Primary. It was some distance to travel each day, but in the country you mixed with everyone. Robert's friend Ed, who often turned up, lived in a home with a dirt floor and his parents could neither read nor write. But at Oakbank that was inconsequential. Ed was loved and always welcome.

Rose had joined her brothers from time to time and dug up her share of the noxious weed, but her main preoccupation was her little cousin. Having neither sisters nor younger siblings, Rose adored Sylvie. Acting as her mother, Rose constantly read stories, sang and played the piano for her. Special animals, birds and other features were pointed out during walks around the station. The response was reciprocal. Before long, the only person Sylvie ever wanted to be with was Rose.

The sandbank still remained a unique attraction, although caution was always required; the fast-flowing current could never be underestimated. But having grown up beside the river, that was not a deterrent. A rope still hung from a large eucalyptus branch, so hours were spent swinging out into the river. If the current ever did take them downstream, they simply swam to the bank and returned along the track. For the Scott boys, swimming in the Murray brought back childhood memories; they, too, loved the sandbank.

Observing Uncle Tam and Aunt Grace respectively help Robert with his reading in the evenings, David shared an experience his brother had undergone at boarding school. Two of Alistair and Jane's grandchildren, Robert MacLeay and William Scott, had hearing difficulties, which hindered literary skills. Curiously, since birth, both had suffered complications with their ears. When William was little, Lottie had spent hours encouraging him to read, but he struggled to cope and it was an ongoing problem. After commencing school in Sydney, Will was asked one day to read aloud in class. He comprehended the words, but performing in public was stressful. Embarrassed and shy, he did the best he could. As he returned to his desk, the teacher announced to the class that his daughter was only in Grade II, but her reading was a hundred times better! Mortified, William hung his head in shame. At dinner in the boarding house that evening, David was shocked at his brother's appearance. Reluctant to disclose the cause of his distress, eventually, under pressure from his brother, William relayed the circumstances. Neither brother was confident, but for David, this was *a bridge too far*. The next day he waited at the classroom door and requested a word with Mr McIntosh. Calmly and courteously, he relayed that his brother, since birth, had suffered hearing impairment, and that reading as well as he did was a significant achievement. No apology was ever given to William, but no further criticism or judgement ever came his way.

Another favourite activity at Oakbank was evening concerts, organised after dinner. When not acting in the various plays, Rose played the piano. Wonderful creativity was involved. The adults loved watching and were very impressed with the talent of these aspiring young actors and the exciting plays, clever sets and costumes they managed to produce from simple items. Occasionally Sylvie was allowed to stay up and participate. However, unsurprisingly, her performances were unpredictable and invariably did not adhere to the script. But usually that just prompted hysterical laughter from both the cast and the audience. The summer Oakbank holiday, while basic, was truly memorable.

In late January, it was time for the Scotts to travel back to Melbourne. Just a few days remained before the brothers returned to Sydney. With great reluctance, they boarded the interstate train. Neither David nor William wished to leave their little sister, nor their uncle and aunt. Their boarding school was too far away. But Cissy hugged them lovingly relaying that although both would be greatly missed, the Easter holidays were just a few weeks away, and then another special holiday could be shared.

Chapter Fifteen

SYLVIE COMMENCED SCHOOL ROUND THE CORNER AND fortunately settled in well. A few weeks later, after collecting her little niece from class, a play in the park was enjoyed, before walking home. An unexpected surprise was waiting when Cissy opened her letterbox. Rarely did they receive overseas mail. But a London stamp and Lady Audrey's handwriting disclosed the source.

Curious to hear about life in England, Cissy enthusiastically opened the letter, but instead a severe shock was revealed. While staying with friends at a castle in Devon, Angus had joined a fox hunt, only to be thrown from his horse. Evidently his mount shied as it approached a fence, bucking and hurling Angus to the ground, where his head hit a log. Death was instant. As Sylvie played with her toys, Cissy sat down in disbelief. She could not accept this reality and so taking Sylvie by the hand, she walked next door to John's practice. He was treating a patient, but she quietly waited till he appeared.

Even before she told him the news, John instantly knew

something profound had occurred. Taking Cissy in his arms, he just held her. A few patients remained, after which he would come straight home. How could Sylvie be told this news? How could her brothers be advised? While Sylvie played with her toys, Cissy, traumatised, lay down on her bed, recalling her mother Jane's wise words: *'Life does not come on our terms.'* After John came home, he distracted Sylvie, as Cissy slowly accepted this terrible reality. Both agreed their little niece be told the next morning and somehow they would advise the Headmaster at the boys' boarding school. Sylvie was fed, read a story and settled for the night. In unbelievable shock, Cissy was barely able to eat any dinner.

Together the Wallaces supported each other. How could they deal with this? After discussion and quiet contemplation, a decision was made that David and William were still at a vulnerable age. For these boys now to accept the loss of their father, as well as their mother, it was essential that a family member be present to communicate this tragedy and support them. Cissy said she would take Sylvie on the train to Sydney and bring the boys home. John agreed in principle, but believed it was too much for his wife. He would accompany her. David and William in due course would return to their former Melbourne school and a home which they loved. There was no alternative.

Early the next morning, John arranged for the doctor who recently had joined his practice, Frederick Black, to attend to his patients and a notice to this effect was placed on the surgery door. Cissy wrote to Tam and her father, relaying the tragic news about Angus. She then took Sylvie to school, delivered her letters at the Post Office and returned to pack for Sydney. After collecting Sylvie, Cissy advised the Principal of Angus' death and of her niece's forthcoming absence due to their Sydney journey to collect her brothers. Then, when they arrived home, Cissy lovingly, while nursing her adored little niece on the couch, relayed the news of her father's tragic accident. Obviously, it was a shock, but Sylvie just clung to her aunt as she rocked her to and fro. She did not weep, but just tranquilly absorbed the reality. It would be more difficult for her brothers, Cissy believed. Sylvie never had spent much time with her father. Other than the Wallaces, her closest and most affectionate associate was Nurse Smith. Early the next morning, John ordered a carriage to Melbourne's City Station where they caught the train to Albury, enabling them to then connect with the New South Wales railway line to Sydney.

An interstate trip was something neither Cissy nor John wished to undertake, but under the circumstances, there was no alternative. Those two young brothers needed love and support. After a long journey, they arrived in Sydney and found their way to Angus' bayside home, where they unpacked and settled in. Previous accommodation in Sydney had never been equal to this. Views across the harbour were breathtaking. The next morning, a carriage transported them to the boys' school where they met with the Headmaster, apprising him of Angus' death. With the boys having no parents, there was, of course, only one option. David and William would accompany their uncle, aunt and little sister to Melbourne where they would re-enrol at their former college.

After hearing the news of their father's accident, the shocked boys packed suitcases and left their boarding school with Uncle John, Aunt Cissy and their little sister. Both were very distressed, but somehow they comforted each other. A carriage delivered everyone, except John, to the harbourside residence. He continued on into the city to meet Angus' solicitor.

Having no expectations, John, and in due course the entire MacLeay family, was agreeably surprised and enormously relieved upon hearing details of Angus' Will and the provision he had made for his children. Although he had chosen to share his life with Lady Audrey, it seemed Angus had finally realised that his new wife lacked filial love and could never be a devoted parent to them. In her care, his children's lives would have been abysmal. Another unexpected positive was that Angus, by reason of his inheritance, was a wealthy man and to ensure honest administration of his estate, he had named Dr John Wallace as his executor. Other than a generous legacy to Lady Audrey, everything was bequeathed to David, William and Sylvie, while a liberal remuneration was to be paid to John, who with Cissy, would be carers of his children, providing them with guidance and sound life values. Contrary to his behaviour after the death of Lottie, these instructions following his fatal riding accident were thoughtful, protective and considerate.

Although all the MacLeays and the Sinclairs had been shocked at Angus' reaction to Lottie's death, when details of his Will were revealed, it appeared that finally his children were at the forefront of his mind. For Lottie's family, it was a relief, and an agreeable surprise. Provision had been made for Lady Audrey, but not at the expense of Angus' children. The large station west of Sydney, a portion of his southern run Mirrimbali, still unsold, and his Sydney home were to be divided equally between his three children. And in the event of his death, the Scott children were to be placed in the care of Dr John Wallace and his wife Cissy.

After visiting Angus' solicitor in George Street, John returned exhausted but nevertheless feeling a satisfied tiredness. Cedric Creighton, a partner in his law firm, appealed to John as a capable and grounded man. Angus was well known to him. Milingil Station might take some time to sell, but fortunately it was not urgent. There were sufficient funds. Cedric knew a Stock and Station Agency in Bathurst. The senior partner was a well-respected man with a reliable reputation and Cedric was confident that in due course Milingil Station would be sold.

To John this was an enormous relief. Mindful of his unattended Elwood practice and the significant responsibility of the three Scott children now placed upon him and his dear wife, he was thankful that the sale of Angus' station west of Sydney and his beautiful harbourside property would be managed by Cedric Creighton. Mirrimbali, on the Murray, also was an issue, but Cedric believed that his firm's Melbourne office could arrange for Angus' Murray River station to be sold as well. Peter Hendrick at the Collins Street office was recommended as the best person to assist John with administration of the estate. Cedric would write and apprise him of the circumstances. Several additional matters in Sydney needed to be addressed before John and Cissy with David, Will and Sylvie boarded the train to Albury. The Scott children had minimal interest in artefacts at the harbourside home. After selling the property, a clearing sale would be arranged. Despite grief for their father, David and William manifested relief and quiet joy to be returning with their sister to their aunt and uncle's home and to their familiar Melbourne school.

When they arrived at Elwood, Alistair was waiting for them. He hugged his grandsons, thinking of Jane and the fortitude she had shown during their life tragedies. Whatever he could do to help was his priority. The Oakbank family sent much love and hoped to see Lottie's trio soon, as did Uncle Duncan and Jess's family.

All three Scott children valued the support and care they were given. Bicycles were bought for David and William as their school was far more distant than Sylvie's. They were so excited. Not returning to Sydney was a huge bonus and how perfect to cycle to school, rather than attend as boarders. A student nearby rode with them. Lunch was packed each day before they headed off. Although it was not expressed in actual terms, David, William and Sylvie felt very sad for their father, but innately they knew that life with their dearly loved aunt and uncle would be loving and beneficial. Since their mother's death, they had spent minimal time together. Now school holidays would be enjoyed at Oakbank with their cousins. It was where the boys had grown up, and time along the Murray River for them was always full of memories. Alistair, their loving grandfather, travelled between his son Tam's Oakbank station and his daughter Cissy's Elwood home, enabling the Scott boys and their little sister to build a special relationship with him when he visited the city.

Chapter Sixteen

As little Sylvie settled into her primary school and David and William returned to their former Melbourne college, the Elwood household established a regular routine. Slowly grief from their father's death diminished. Refreshingly, reality was discussed, rather than kept hidden and unspoken, which never would have been the case with their stepmother. Both boys and Sylvie questioned Aunty Cissy about their parents, dearly loved Lottie and their father Angus, as well as Lady Audrey. While not always easy, Cissy, mindful of her mother Jane, knew there was only ever one story – the truth, which she gently and lovingly shared, to the best of her ability.

Having adored their Christmas holiday on the Murray with Uncle Tam and Aunty Grace, David asked if perhaps Easter could be spent there. Cissy wrote to her brother Tam, who instantly replied, yes, his family would love their cousins to visit again. Although now cooler in Melbourne than in the North, summer had been exceptionally hot, with minimal rain. In late March, the Scott brothers knew it would still be warm enough to swim in the Murray. When Term 1 ended, suitcases were excitedly packed. Cissy knew they would all love Oakbank, and that Sylvie would be cared for by her brothers, as well as Rose. Elwood would be quiet without their loving trio, but the Easter holidays offered a quiet respite for John and Cissy after the trauma of Angus' death and the consequent change in their lifestyle. So they drove their carriage to the city and waved goodbye to Sylvie and her brothers as they boarded a train to the Murray. Their grandfather, Alistair had returned to the bush a few weeks earlier.

After several stops along the way, the Scotts finally reached Echuca. Waiting at the station for them were Uncle Tam and his daughter Rose. Sylvie's excitement when she saw her cousin was special. She raced across the platform, hugging Rose with much joy. Climbing onto Uncle Tam's cart, they circuited the town and crossed the river, before driving out to Oakbank. The countryside now looked so much drier than in December and it was suffocatingly hot. Rose told her cousins that during the last couple of months, with excessive heat and no rain, the only way to cool off was dipping into the river. That was exactly what David and William were looking forward to, as well as swinging on the special rope at the sandbank.

Unlike at Christmas, the boys this time had no expectation of a luxurious vacation. They knew it would be sleeves rolled up and hard work. But how much better than school holidays in the city. Sure enough, after unpacking their cases and enjoying a fun catch-up with Richard and Robert down by the river, dinner was served and Uncle Tam asked if tomorrow the boys please might rise early, since he wished to move a large herd of cattle. At the manager's request, Tam's mob had been roaming on a stretch of Mirrimbali land, in a bid to eat down the pasture. With the remaining acreage for sale, and almost all livestock sold, Tam readily had accepted this offer, since there was minimal feed on Oakbank, and reducing the Mirrimbali grass, also would be beneficial. But now it was time for drovers to bring the cattle home.

The six cousins slept in beds arranged along a partly closed-in veranda, not dissimilar to the Mirrimbali one. These sleep-outs were common features in country homesteads. Sometimes flies and mosquitoes, which somehow got through the flywire, were a nuisance, but at least a breeze, although not always cool, flowed through at night.

In accordance with Uncle Tam's request, at daybreak, the four boys rose. Aunty Grace had already prepared breakfast. Awakened by their brothers, Rose and Sylvie joined them at the kitchen table. Although not participating in the round-up, the girls followed their brothers to the stockyards and watched as they mounted horses and galloped off, leaving a trail of dust in their wake. Hot and grimy, Rose took little Sylvie's hand, ran into the house and grabbed two towels, before skipping down to the river and along to the sandbank. Even though Sylvie could swim, Rose did not let go of her hand. The current was too strong. Into the shallow water they dipped, washed themselves, feeling the lovely fresh sand beneath their feet, before spreading out on towels and relaxing in the sun. An hour of leisure was enjoyed, before suddenly, a very strong wind unexpectedly came from the South. It was so fierce that lying on the sand was not only impossible, it was dangerous. As well as leaves, sticks picked up in the blast flew through the air. The girls straight away gathered their belongings and walked back to the house.

David and Will had galloped down the Oakbank driveway after their cousins Richard and Robert, turning right outside the gate along the dirt road towards the unsold section of the Scotts' property, where Tam's cattle were grazing. The Mirrimbali homestead and most of the land had a new owner, but still a portion, familiar to the boys, remained. However, usual access via the front driveway was no longer possible. About half a mile further down the road, they opened a gate and cantered into a fenced off paddock. Unlike Oakbank, Mirrimbali now had boundaries. Angus Scott had arranged for barbed wire fences to be constructed on both his stations. Tam would love to have done the same but, of course, he could not afford it. Fortunately, his periphery with Mirrimbali had been secured, which was a huge bonus. Richard and Robert had helped their father construct one fence beyond the homestead, but much more was required.

After opening the gate and entering the paddock, the boys quietly trotted down the left side, towards the river, where the bulk of the herd had clustered. Not wanting to startle the cattle, they progressed slowly. Both Robert and Richard held stock-whips. The cousins followed in their wake. Robert's instructions were that after reaching the river they must spread out and unhurriedly guide the cattle up towards the dirt road. Then before the herd got too near the gate, Robert would ride on ahead, blocking the southern route, ensuring the wayward beasts headed back to Oakbank.

Not only was the heat stifling, but as Rose and Sylvie had observed, a very strong south-easterly wind had blown up, causing debris to fly through the air. With the gate to the roadway open, the vast herd could not be abandoned, so the riders spread out ensuring control. Suddenly without warning, Blackjack, William's horse, started bucking, shying and trying to dismount his rider. Whether it was the wild wind or minimal training was unclear, but Richard and Robert were shocked, both offering to switch mounts. Will, an experienced rider, assured them he could manage. Richard threw across his stock-whip, but still Blackjack continued to buck and rear. The other three spread out, slowly edging the mob forward. With the gate to the road open, the stock had to be controlled. A struggle was ahead for William, but he would not submit.

Unable to follow the others, he decided the best ploy was to exhaust his rebellious mount. At the cracking of his whip, Blackjack was forced to charge ahead. The wild stallion bolted along the upper bank of the river, with William holding on for dear life. Richard and Robert glanced back anxiously, but David assured them that Will would survive. No horse could unseat his brother. Given free rein, Blackjack galloped unrestricted, before finally halting, exhausted, as the Mirrimbali homestead came into view. Here were so many memories for Will, but there was no time to absorb them. Taking a tight grip of the reins, he straight away cracked the whip, forcing his defiant stallion to return, back along the path they had just ridden. Blackjack was worn out, but refusing this rebellious steed any respite, William drove him relentlessly onwards, until finally they joined the other three horsemen herding the mob towards the exit along the dusty road to Oakbank. The black stallion was depleted. Having always thought of their city cousins as somewhat spoilt and indulged, Richard and Robert were very impressed. Will's ride had been an extraordinary performance. Time and effort to break in and control Blackjack was now not required. The spirit of this wild stallion had been conquered by their fearless cousin.

Slowly the herd ambled along the track, until finally Uncle Tam came into view, standing well back along the road with his cattle flogger and dogs, to ensure the cattle entered the open gateway into Oakbank. Through they went, past the homestead, eventually entering a paddock on the western side of the property. The availability of pasture, albeit dry, at Mirrimbali had been invaluable to Tam. Grass on his property was at a very low ebb. Hopefully some autumn rain soon would fall. Eventually, as the last couple of cows followed their leaders into the parched acreage, Robert lifted across the wooden railings ensuring closure. It was now just after midday but all four were weary. Dismounting, they released the equally tired horses into the house paddock before heading to the homestead.

Chapter Seventeen

WORRYINGLY, THE WIND NOW WAS AT GALE FORCE. Leaving their boots at the back door, the lads headed in to wash and change for Aunty Grace's lunch, after which they planned a refreshing swim down by the sandbank. It was almost hotter inside than out! While eating and chatting round the table, Robert commented that he could smell smoke. No one took much notice, until Alistair left the table and walked out the back door. There was definitely more than a smell of smoke. Walking round the homestead and down to the river, Alistair could see not only smoke but flames across the Murray in the distance. Clearly the frontage opposite Mirrimbali was alight. Thank God they were on the north side of the river, with minimal native trees. Throughout Alistair and Jane's many years on the riverbank, they and their family had always felt safe. In addition to being on the north side of the river, there was, thankfully, not too much to ignite around Mirrimbali, or the adjacent Oakbank homestead, now Tam and Grace's. But the exception today was gale force winds. Months of heat, drought, and bushfires had been survived in former days, but if wind from this inferno blew sparks onto the property, serious danger lay ahead.

Down at the water's edge Alistair could see in the distance two men on the wharf at Mirrimbali filling buckets and running back towards the homestead. Joining his father, Tam immediately directed his sons and their cousins to grab buckets or whatever they could find from the shed or elsewhere, fill them and then drench the house as best they could. He then broke branches from a deciduous tree in order to lash flames, if or when the fire reached Oakbank. Alistair joined the boys, but Tam called out, *'Father, please go into the house and take care of Grace and the girls. It's too dangerous for you out here.'* But before Alistair could enter the house, Grace, Rose and Sylvie rushed out to see what was happening. *'Please, get woollen blankets and go straight to the dam,'* instructed Tam.

Whilst this had never occurred before, Grace knew exactly what to do. Taking Sylvie's hand, Rose followed her mother inside, collecting blankets before rushing down to the dam. With only about a foot of water remaining after the long drought and an excessively hot summer, the dam was really just a quagmire but, of course, it was safer than the house. Grace submerged one blanket in the dirty water before placing it beside Rose and Sylvie sitting among the reeds. Then, after drenching hers, she joined them at the edge of the dam. Barely had they grasped the situation, when hopping across before their eyes went several kangaroos, with little joeys following in their wake. *'Oh, I hope the poor cattle will be safe,'* cried Grace. *'Unlike the kangaroos, they cannot get out!'*

Grace wanted to join Tam in the bid to save their property, but first and foremost she had to protect Rose and Sylvie. *'If, or when, the fire engulfs the homestead,'* she told the girls, *'you must wade into the middle of the shallow dam, and place these saturated woollen blankets across your head and shoulders, and completely cover yourselves.'* This would be the safest course of action, since there would be minimal chance of the damp wool igniting. Alistair, she expected would join them. Tam again directed his father to care for the girls, saying, *'This situation is too dangerous, father,'* but Alistair insisted on combating the fire in whatever way he could.

The smoke and heat were horrendous, to say nothing of the wild wind. They might escape flames, but would they survive suffocation? It was terrifying! Tam, with his father, sons and nephews, clutching buckets and other containers, continued to scoop up water from the river, carrying it up the bank, before hurling it over the house, as high as they could reach. After soaking the lower level, Robert and Richard dragged across an old wooden bench from the shed, which they stood on, enabling them to throw the water higher to protect the homestead.

When they were down at the water's edge, after soaking almost all the house, it became clear that the bushfire had crossed the river and that possibly Jack Henderson's property was alight. Sky high flames definitely appeared to be on the north side, but dense smoke now blocked out everything. *'Poor Jack and his family,'* said Tam. *'I do hope they are safe.'* Cameron had moved to Brisbane, but Jack and Miriam still lived on the property. Like Alistair, Jack loved his life there, still working as hard as he could, with his son Clive undertaking the heavy lifting.

Although the river was a source of security in the worst possible scenario, many eucalyptus trees, which were highly flammable, grew along the bank, hence Tam's recommendation of the dam even though it was shallow and muddy. After drenching the homestead, the men then carried buckets of water across to the shed, applying the same procedure. David and Will were devastated. In Sydney, they had observed fire carts attend a shocking blaze. In addition to tanks on horse-drawn wagons, hoses were used to quell the flames, but sadly Uncle Tam had no such equipment. It was very frightening, but all they could do was help their uncle during this terrifying ordeal.

If only the wind would drop, but it grew wilder and stronger. Horrified, the Oakbank household strained their eyes in an attempt to establish where exactly the fire was centred. In addition to blinding and suffocating smoke, crackling timber communicated imminent danger. It seemed that possibly both Jack Henderson's and the Mirrimbali shearing sheds were alight. Whether the extensive lawn surrounding the old neighbouring homestead would protect it, remained to be seen. Flying sparks could ignite anything instantly. How far would this bushfire spread? Tam recalled masses of highly flammable hay bales stored in the Mirrimbali shed. Thank heavens all his hay had been eaten. The density of the smoke was suffocating and blinding, but the four young cousins, with Tam and their grandfather, continued drenching the shed.

Robert suddenly realised that a cattle trough could be useful for water cartage. He and Richard quickly harnessed a mare to the cart and then loaded the trough onto it, before leading the somewhat intimidated horse down to the river. With all the team working, the trough was quickly filled and carted across to the Mirrimbali fence, where water was tipped across the grass along the boundary. Sparks flying through the air could not be stopped, but they hoped spreading water might defend this vulnerable area. It seemed like a drop in the ocean, but anything to stop the encroaching inferno was beneficial. The heat and smoke were unbearable. Turns were taken with the trough-laden cart while the exhausted mare was replaced with another horse. Gradually grass along the fence line was saturated.

Unsurprisingly, flames from the Mirrimbali blaze soon could be seen spreading across the dry grass towards Oakbank. Branches which Tam had broken from the deciduous tree were grabbed, as the boys raced towards the boundary, preparing to slash flames as they spread along the grass. The water cartage continued. It was terrifying, but this inferno somehow had to be kept at bay. At least along the barbed wire boundary there were no trees, just bare dry grass. Would the dripped water have any effect? They hoped just some of the burning grass might be kept at bay. At least Tam's pasture, after the drought, was threadbare, limiting ignition.

Further north, along the fence line towards the road, Richard suddenly noticed that flames had crept under the fence and were spreading quickly. Racing there, the boys slashed the burning grass with branches, and stamped on it with their boots. Robert straight away led the horse to this ignited site with the next trough of water, and continued soaking the extended area. Progress was slow, but thankfully their combined efforts gradually reduced the fire's spread. Walking past his labouring father, sons and nephews, Tam put his arms round them, thanking everyone wholeheartedly, wondering where he might be without their brave and tireless support. They were all doing an incredible and heroic job. His gratitude knew no bounds.

Confident that Rose would take good care of Sylvie, Grace briefly left the girls and raced into the house. She fetched water and food, packing it into a basket, which she took across the paddock, placing it on the ground near the hard-working men. Helpless and terrified, she hugged Tam whispering that all she could do by the dam was pray, hoping that perhaps his dear mother Jane might be listening.

The boys battled on for hours, incredibly relieved that,

just for the moment, Oakbank was not alight. Eventually, as dusk was approaching, the force of the wind began to diminish, bringing enormous relief. Robert continued leading the horse and cart to the river, refilling the trough and spreading water. There was no thought of slowing down, or easing this ongoing fight. It would be days before any sense of safety could be assumed. However, soaking grass along the boundary had definitely been effective. The entire fence line adjacent to the fire had been drenched, but with minimal relief from the heat, the routine continued. Other than overhead sparks, this was the most dangerous section and the battle would continue throughout the night.

Mirrimbali Station occupied a sizeable area of land, including the picturesque U-bend in front of the homestead, which had enamoured Jane and Alistair on their arrival from Scotland. Unquestionably, it was a unique location, with the Murray providing boundaries on three sides of the property. The bend in front of the homestead, facing Victoria to the South was not extensive, but land along the East and west stretched for considerable distances beside the fast-flowing river. Oakbank, further downstream, had just one water frontier. While not on the scale of Mirrimbali, it still provided a beautiful outlook across the Murray. From the top of the riverbank, Tam initially could view the raging fire, but dense smoke had soon made that impossible. Thankfully, there was considerable distance between the neighbouring shearing sheds and his boundary. Unfortunately, nothing could be certain, but scorching heat and thick smoke indicated there now was a substantial inferno on the north side of the river. Tam's instinct was that both stations were alight, ensuring nothing would stop his battle to save Oakbank. How were the Hendersons? Jack's property further upstream was not too far from the Mirrimbali stockyards.

Having stayed with Rose and Sylvie in the reeds beside the dam, Grace decided, once the wind dropped, to leave the muddy woollen blankets draped across their wire clothesline, ready to seize in an emergency, and take the girls inside. The extra dry blankets she placed beside the front door. Presently the greatest relief was no wind.

Settling the girls, Grace then packed fresh water, sandwiches and fruit into a basket, before rushing outside to deliver more supplies to her brave, exhausted firefighters. But hurrying down the front steps, with shock, she suddenly saw a blackened figure staggering up the riverbank towards her. Dumping the supplies, Grace sped down to help him. Despite having swum quite some distance, the fugitive's face and body were black with soot. He was severely burnt.

'Oh my God, Clive! Please, just hold my arm and come inside.' Barely recognisable, it was Clive Henderson, severely scorched and seriously injured. Placing immense pressure on Grace, he managed to stumble up to the house, before collapsing on the veranda. Unable to lift him, Grace opened the front door and called to Rose. *'Please, darling, run and*

find father. Clive Henderson is severely injured. We need help!'
Heeding her mother, Rose sped off in search of her father.

Sitting beside Clive, Grace soothed him with her gentle voice, tenderly stroking his hair. However, before Rose returned with Tam, galloping hooves were heard. Uncle Duncan and Stuart had ridden across from Argyll. Living further downstream, they luckily had avoided the bushfire, but concerned for Tam's family, they had galloped over to help. Observing a body beside Grace, they dismounted, hobbled the horses, and raced to her aid, presuming it to be her husband or one of her sons. Horrified, they stared at Clive. Of course, they knew him well. He was Jess's cousin. However, his face was so badly disfigured that it took them a minute to recognise him. Stuart straight away offered to carry him inside. Grace opened the door to Alistair's room where he was carefully placed on the bed. With a bowl of warm water, Grace gently sponged him. Suffering horrendous burns, Clive remained unconscious.

Seeing Rose running across the paddock, Tam straight away left the men, returning to the homestead with his daughter. His sons, Richard and Robert, with their cousins David, Will, and his father, Alistair, continued the vigilant battle. A single spark could instantly ignite trees, grass or timber structures, causing irreparable damage, but thankfully the wind had diminished, which was a huge relief.

Already shattered by the day's events, Tam entered the room, staring in disbelief at his barely recognisable friend and neighbour. Within seconds he slipped down on his knees, before stretching out on the floor. Anxious, Grace knelt beside her husband, but he calmly assured her he was fine. He just needed time. The vision of Clive's scorched and blackened body had caused him to feel faint. After an enduring battle amid suffocating heat and smoke, it was not surprising. Fighting the blaze, Tam had thought what a blessing it was that John and Cissy had not accompanied the Scott trio, but seeing Clive, all Tam could think of was how valuable his brother-in-law John's medical skills now would be. How could they help! Transporting Clive to the local hospital, even via the river, would be a risk, not only for the patient, but for his aides as well.

Tam remained on the floor for some time; then, after sipping water, he rose to his feet. Uncle Duncan and Stuart, equally shocked, asked how they might ameliorate Clive's dreadful state. It was sadly acknowledged that nothing could be done. Clive's injuries were beyond healing. The bushfire, however, still remained a serious threat, so ensuring Grace could cope, Duncan and his son Stuart joined Tam, as he emotionally returned to the fire front. Observing the food basket on the veranda, where Grace had dumped it as she assisted Clive, Stuart carried it across, to share with the night watchers. The last image of their scorched neighbour would never be forgotten.

Grace gently and lovingly comforted Clive with her soothing voice, but soon after the men left, Clive died, never regaining consciousness. Worried about both his dying neighbour and his wife, Tam soon returned. Grace had done everything she possibly could. Tam held her in his arms, before covering Clive's body and joining his wife in a prayer that their friend might now rest in peace. Night had settled in. Tam carried Clive's body over to the shed, where he laid it out respectfully, until arrangements for his burial could be made. Grace was shattered, but as her exhausted husband pointed out, how fortunate had they been, so far, to have escaped the inferno. Also, in light of Clive's horrendous injuries, perhaps it was best that he hadn't survived. Ongoing life could never have been normal, while the pain would be excruciating. What exactly had happened at Amaru, and where were Jack and Miriam?

Grace checked the girls, who after a light snack were now in bed. She then prepared more food and water for the firefighters. She passed the basket to Tam, who held his wife in an enduring hug, thanking her for all she had done, before setting off with more refreshments for the boys, who were still carefully guarding their threatened boundary. With Uncle Duncan and Stuart, the night watch now comprised eight.

The Sinclairs participated in this defensive vigil for several hours. Then, acknowledging the amazing preventative achievement their cousins had accomplished, they felt reasonably confident that Oakbank temporarily was safe, and decided to ride home, to protect Argyll and their family. Clive's death needed to be relayed to Jess, as well as the unknown fate of Amaru. Stuart asked Tam if he would like him to ride back in the morning and accompany him to Uncle Jack's property? Since Argyll was quite a long way downstream, Tam replied that if Oakbank seemed safe in the morning, he would ride to Jack's with one of his sons and relay the news of Clive's tragic death to his parents. They then could establish what help was required and check the extent of damage suffered there. Tam heartily thanked his uncle and cousin for their thoughtful and generous support, before settling in with the boys for what remained of a long, sleepless night, on constant watch. Outbreaks still could occur at any time.

Faint moonlight guided Duncan and his son, as they mounted their horses. Because the route was covered in dense smoke, it was a slow ride, but thankfully when eventually they reached Argyll, their property and homestead were safe. Not only was Argyll some distance away, it was also beyond a further bend in the river, which fortunately had been unscathed by the fire.

Drained physically and emotionally after such an horrendous day, Tam relayed Clive's tragic fate to the men on watch. His death was unspeakable, to say nothing of the unknown fate of his parents. The frightening reality, nevertheless, reinforced how fortunate they were to have survived. It was also a prudent reminder that ongoing vigilance was crucial. Bushfires, as they all had witnessed, were unpredictable and in many cases unstoppable.

Exhausted, Alistair accepted that nothing more could be contributed by him and finally agreeing to his son's request, he trudged back to the homestead. Unaware that dying Clive had spent his final tortured hours suffering in his bed, Alistair slipped between fresh sheets, thoughtfully replaced by Grace. What a day! Exhausted as he was, sleep was in abeyance, as he lay contemplating not just the terrifying day but also his extraordinary life. Nothing was certain, but he felt reasonably confident that the brave and fearless defence mounted today by his son and grandsons would ensure the ongoing safety of Oakbank. As a child, Alistair hated the freezing, snow-covered winters in the north of Scotland. During those icy months, tragic deaths had occurred. Australia always seemed to be the lucky country, but today that view had been reversed. Wild storms sailing on the *Esperance* were terrifying, but nothing Alistair ever had experienced compared with today's petrifying and unstoppable inferno. Oakbank had been a hair's breadth from being a blackened ruin. What a brave and courageous job those young men had done, halting the raging bushfire and preventing it from destroying everything the young MacLeay family possessed. The other frightening issue was no forewarning! One moment the day was calm and sunny, the next minute their lives could have vanished in seconds.

Daybreak appeared across the eastern horizon after a long, tense night. With no new outbreaks, a sense of relief enveloped the boys. However, nothing could be certain, so warily they stretched out along the Mirrimbali boundary and right round the Oakbank property, some on horseback and some on foot, checking for any vulnerable sites. The chance of rain was remote, but at least there was minimal wind. Bare paddocks, with token pasture, was another positive.

When eventually they reassembled at their overnight location to discuss respective observations regarding danger points, Robert said he would continue soaking the grass along the boundary, where the risk was greatest. The others would support him, remaining alert for any outbreak. It was another very hot day, but at least there was no wind. As they headed down to the river, to help reload the trough, a distant whistle could be heard, followed by a call. Dense smoke still enveloped the property, but emerging through the haze a Mirrimbali workman appeared at the fence. Joining him at their boundary, Tam introduced Bert to his father and nephews. Like Clive Henderson's, Bert's face, clothes and hands were black, but he, luckily, was uninjured. The homestead miraculously had been spared, but the shearing shed, yards and every other structure on Mirrimbali had been burnt. Two lads guarding the burning rubble were also unscathed. But what 24 hours of hell had it been! *'How is Oakbank?'* Bert asked. Amaru, the entire Hendersons' property, he believed had been burnt to the ground. This of course could not be verified, because it was impossible to see through the smoke. But Bert was very concerned because despite whistling and calling out, no one had responded.

Tam told Bert that he couldn't imagine what might have happened to his family or his property without the extraordinary contribution of his sons, nephews and father. Their help had been invaluable. Grace's tragic story of finding Clive Henderson, then was relayed. Tam believed the current must have carried Clive downstream to Oakbank, since the possibility of swimming with his shocking injuries would have been limited. Somehow, he had managed to reach the bank and drag himself up. Clive's body, he told Bert, had been temporarily laid to rest in his shed, but as soon as Oakbank was safe, he would ride over to Jack's, relay the tragic news and establish Clive's family's wishes regarding his burial. Bert responded, *'Because the fire was so fierce, I reckon no one there has survived.'* Nothing could be seen through the thick black smoke.

Mirrimbali's new owner was not in residence. He apparently was a wealthy financial investor in Melbourne. In some respects, the description of him reminded Alistair of Hugh Mortimer, the original owner and creator of the spectacular Murray River estate. Bert and two other workmen maintained the station for him. Since the recent sale, just a few sheep grazed there, but sadly they all had perished as fire ravaged the property. How fortunate was Tam that the boys had brought back his cattle yesterday, and then battled the inferno throughout the afternoon and night! Where would Oakbank be without them!

The Hendersons at Amaru were at the forefront of his

mind, but for Tam it was a case of first things first, namely his family's safety and, of course, their property. After riding round Oakbank and confirming the boys' appraisal that temporarily it seemed secure from the fire, he decided that his sons, Richard and Robert, with his father and nephew Will, would remain on watch, while his nephew David accompanied him to convey the tragic news to Clive's family. The scorched body lying in his shed could not be ignored.

Indoors, Rose helped her mother cook and sustain the household. Fortunately, vegetables from the garden and fruit from the orchard had been collected by the girls prior to the fire. Watching Rose climb fruit trees to reach ripe peaches, apricots and apples, Sylvie tried to copy her, but it was too dangerous. *'Maybe next year when you are taller and stronger you will be able to help me,'* Rose said. Soup, a casserole, cakes and biscuits were made. Sylvie, of course, could not do much, but Rose gave her small tasks and encouraged her accomplishments. When her brothers witnessed their little sister in her kitchen apron, serving freshly made biscuits and other produce, they were overjoyed. If only their mother could see her little daughter!

Dense smoke still covered the property as far as the eye could see. After saddling horses in the mounting yards, Tam and David trotted off down the driveway, to the Hendersons'. Going slowly was their only option. Dense smoke limited vision while the outside road was a hazard. Huge scorched branches had fallen across the track, while dead koalas, wombats and possums littered the route. It was devastating. Kangaroos, it seemed, had escaped. *'I cannot believe we survived,'* Tam said. The fire on Mirrimbali had crossed the road, burning fences and land further to the north. How Oakbank had been spared was a miracle! Tam's additional manpower had been invaluable.

Several miles down the road, they reached the entrance to Jack's property. On hand for his uncle, David was mindful of the tragic news to be relayed to Clive's parents. Their vision was limited by thick smoke, but familiar with Amaru, Tam knew a second gate on the left provided access to the homestead. However, as they approached this entrance, it was more than apparent that unutterable carnage had occurred here. Live coals were burning as they rode past the stockyards. The two-storey home which overlooked the river was just a smouldering ruin. The remainder of a brick chimney was the only thing standing. Tam had anticipated damage, but nothing on this scale. Where were Jack and Miriam? Had they fled like Clive or were their remains among the smoking ruins. David also was in disbelief. The scene was unspeakable. Neither had ever seen anything like it. There was not even anywhere to safely strap the horses. Nothing had survived the inferno.

Eventually Tam recalled a metal stump near the river, where they managed to safely secure their steeds. It seemed that the purpose of their visit, to relay tragic tidings, most likely would not be required. After securing the horses, Tam and David set off to establish what might have happened to the Hendersons. It was horrifying, and hazardous. Live coals still burned everywhere. Reaching the homestead, they carefully stepped through the wreckage. Most of the house was still smouldering, so there was a serious risk of getting burnt. Warily investigating further, they came across the remains of what must have been Miriam. A silver pendant identified her.

Scouring through the rest of the charred wreckage revealed nothing. Luckily neither suffered burns. Feeling disgusted and believing he might vomit, David walked through the rubble towards the river, seating himself on the bank and placing his head in his hands. Tam searched the shed and the yards, but only burning ruins remained there. After a rest, David walked upstream along the bank before cutting across towards the smouldering stockyards to join Uncle Tam. However, passing the blackened dairy revealed another dreadful shock, the body of Jack. This, it appeared, had been his last stand, fighting the bushfire as it ignited the milking shed. Absolutely nothing could be done. Sheep in the adjacent blackened paddock were dead, their carcases spread out across the burnt expanse, whilst chickens in their pen, and dairy cows had been scorched to death. It was a nightmare.

Tam asked his nephew if he still felt sick. David replied yes, but that he would manage. This shocking disaster must immediately be reported, Tam told him. Cameron Henderson lived in Brisbane with his family, so there was no way of communicating with him. This was a police matter. Right now, Tam said, he must ride to the township and report these three deaths, and the circumstances, in so far as he knew them. *'Are you well enough to ride back to Oakbank?'* he asked. David reassured him that he was. An apology for subjecting his nephew to such an horrendous situation was made, as well as acknowledgement of his support. Distressing and dreadful though it had been, David said he was glad he had accompanied Uncle Tam, rather than leaving him to face this shocking sight alone. Again, a sobering reality for them both was how fortunate they had been to survive. This was the worst scenario either had ever seen. The horses were untied and mounted, then on reaching the outside road, they set off in different directions. As Tam turned his horse towards the distant township, he waved goodbye to David, who on his mount quietly ambled along the charred track. There would be no haste. Time to absorb this recent horror was needed, as well as caution to avoid the numerous hazards on the road.

Turning into the home driveway, David was aware that his brother and cousins were still hard at work endeavouring to protect Oakbank. They needed his contribution, but time to come to terms with the devastation just witnessed at Amaru was essential. He still felt sick. Unsaddling his horse, he released it into the house paddock, before walking down to sit on the riverbank. Viewing the fast-flowing stream where he had grown up was always therapeutic. Closing his eyes, he quietly meditated, thinking of his childhood and his dead father and mother. Life wasn't fair, but it was still good and one must never give up. His life and that of Will and Sylvie had been difficult, but the last few days, somehow, had put everything into perspective. Heartbreaks had been suffered, but also, there had been many blessings. A wise teacher, Mr Kent, always had advised that one must focus on the positives, not the negatives. How many people around the world had experienced the innumerable benefits and opportunities he had received? Never had he or his siblings been short of food, or clothing and always they had lived in warm, comfortable homes. A good education had been provided and despite losing their parents, no one could have been better carers than Aunt Cissy and Uncle John, Uncle Tam and Aunty Grace. Mr Kent's other sound advice was that, as the eldest brother, he must be a good role model for his younger siblings.

The vision of Jack and Miriam Henderson continued in the forefront of his mind. The bushfire had engulfed that family within minutes, while records and memories of their lives had disappeared with them. David lay down on the sand. Thinking of Mr Kent, another valuable memory surfaced, one never far from his mind. It was Aiden, his Sydney school friend. Each morning Aiden's mother walked with him to school and collected him in the afternoon. Aiden was clever, but tragically he had been born with minimal vision. David always spent a lot of time with him, both in class and at recreation. Aiden was an inspiration. He never complained and somehow coped when cruel students bullied him. How wise was Mr Kent? If ever David was tempted to feel sorry for himself, he would remember Aiden. What courage that boy always had shown, despite being afflicted with the cruellest impairment. Feeling restored and stronger after this quiet, contemplative spell, David left the bank and went in search of the boys. Relaying the Hendersons' dreadful fate would not be easy, but his quiet time on the riverbank had definitely restored and strengthened him.

Entering the town, Tam rode straight to the Police Station. He was still in shock, but there was no alternative to this terrible reality. It had to be recorded. With the police's authorisation, burial had to be arranged for Clive and his parents, while Cameron in Brisbane must be notified. Tam hoped the police would agree to Clive's immediate interment. How the horrendous carnage at Amaru might be cleaned up was beyond him. It was over to the constabulary, or perhaps the Hendersons' solicitor.

By the time Tam arrived home, dusk was approaching, but he felt a sense of relief that, to the best of his ability, he had done all he could for the Henderson family. The Police Officer was appreciative of Tam's tragic, but important information. Jack's solicitor would be contacted, who would inform Cameron, while administration of the annihilated Amaru estate, also, would be undertaken by him. Another huge relief was that the policeman said he would arrange transport to Oakbank in the morning to collect Clive's body and those of his parents at Amaru. A burial and commemorative service for the Henderson family would be organised by their solicitor, in conjunction with their surviving son. Tam also reported the significant carnage spread along the road. Support within the town to clear the track, would be arranged by the police as well. Although exhausted from his ride, Tam felt a sense of fulfilment. Those matters had to be recorded. But regrettably there was no way he could join the boys tonight on bushfire watch. Utterly depleted, he still was covered in dirt and soot, so Grace filled their tub with water heated on the stove, enabling her dear husband to sponge and clean himself, which would contribute to a well-deserved night's sleep. When eventually Oakbank was safe and the boys returned to their sleep-out beds, Grace would do the same for them. However, in order to cool off and clean themselves, the young lads earlier had dipped into the river. How refreshing, as always, it had been!

Grace said if she had known Tam was going into the township, she would have given him her letter for Cissy. The Scott brothers were due back at school in two days, but in light of what had happened, with dense smoke everywhere and the bushfire possibly still active, the entire household agreed that it would be in everyone's best interests if they remained for an extra week. Straight after breakfast, Grace rode to their entrance where she awaited a young man who lived a few miles away. Each morning he cantered past on his way to work. Sure enough, before long, trotting hooves were heard and Dick, observing Grace, slackened pace and rode across to speak with her. His office was just a couple of doors from the Post Office, so her letter would be posted first thing. Dick shared his relief that their mutual families had survived. Acknowledging Grace's appreciation, Dick then said that seeing her always was a pleasure and, as usual, she had brightened up his day. News of the terrible bushfire doubtless would be in the Melbourne newspapers by now, so for Cissy to be reassured they were all safe and to know that Sylvie and her brothers would be staying for an extra week, would be a relief.

No rain came, but the temperature dropped and the next few nights were just a little cooler with minimal wind, which reinforced their safety. Uncle Tam was given lots of support on the property during the remaining week, while swims at the sandbank, also were enjoyed. It was then time for suitcases to be packed and the Scott children to return to Melbourne. Heartfelt goodbyes were shared, before Uncle Tam harnessed his mare and drove his niece and nephews to the station. Grandy chose to stay with Tam and his family, hoping he could continue to be of some use. It had been an unbelievably stressful time, but once again the Scott boys, in the presence of their MacLeay cousins, had coped in a strong and mature way and had been of invaluable help to their uncle.

Chapter Eighteen

NESTLED NEXT TO DAVID ON THE TRAIN, SYLVIE FELL INTO a deep sleep. The long return journey provided ample time for the brothers to talk and share their innermost feelings. It had been a frightening, stressful and extraordinary Easter, but as with so many life experiences, especially ones on the Murray River, the boys had not only survived, but also in some ways felt empowered by the bushfire and its consequences. Not many people ever would experience such a terrifying inferno, let alone survive it. Uncle Tam and Grandy had been amazing, to say nothing of their cousins, Robert and Richard. That their mother's brother, Duncan, and his son Stuart, had ridden from Argyll to help, was also memorable. Their family was special.

Fortunately, neither of the boys had actually seen Clive Henderson in the final stages of his agonising death, but David's description of the devastation on their property and the bodies of Jack and Miriam was something no one ever would choose to witness. Describing blackened Amaru, David was very surprised when Will said that he, too, had been there. *'Are you serious?'* he asked. *'Why on earth would you go there?'* After the fire had settled and the police had collected Clive's body at Oakbank and his parents' bodies at ravaged Amaru, Will asked cousin Richard if he would agree to ride over to the devastated property with him. After they had completed their morning circuit and ensured Oakbank's safety, Richard agreed.

They cantered down the road which had been marginally cleared of the bushfire debris, but on entry to Amaru, they, like David, were very shocked. At no stage did they dismount. Will's main wish was to thoroughly survey the site. Surprisingly, there was only one dam, nowhere near the homestead, which undoubtedly increased vulnerability to the sudden and unexpected conflagration. Listening to his brother, David again shuddered, recalling his horror at finding the scorched Hendersons. Will, having seen the carnage, empathised with his brother, but was thankful that his perspective had been distant. The Easter bushfire would leave lifelong excruciating memories, but there was something cathartic about expressing trauma rather than supressing it.

As the train rattled along, it became evident that their distressing Easter had been extensively discussed and now was put to rest, but never would it be forgotten. David then commenced to reveal his future prospects, since this was his final school year. Like Uncle John, he was gravitating towards medicine. Whether his results would admit him to the faculty remained to be seen, but innately that profession appealed. Quietly he mused on this choice, or whether perhaps law or another career might be better? Surely making a difference in people's lives would be fulfilling.

Will listened, allowing David to express his thoughts. In time it would be clear which path his brother should take. At no stage did Will interrupt or question him. The Scott brothers were close, but very different. David was academic, having always succeeded at school. A university course was definitely his future. For Will, school had been a struggle. With his hearing problems, education overall had been challenging, but his older brother had always supported him. A talented sportsman, Will had performed skilfully in whichever team he had participated, but underlying this ability, was a lack of confidence. Unlike in other families where rivalry among siblings was pronounced, the Scott brothers were not competitive. Their interests and talents were so diverse that never had there been any jealously between them. Observing Will's difficulties at school, David encouraged and shielded him. Their bond was strong, while Will, mindful of his brother's support, was equally on hand for David. Three significant factors in their closeness were: their much younger sister, their mother's death at Sylvie's birth and their father's long absences from respective homes. Without parents to guide them, life had not been easy, but a close and loving bond had emanated. Anyone familiar with them, perceived that.

After David shared thoughts about his future, Will spoke up, certainly surprising his brother. This Easter holiday had influenced him towards a passion nurtured since childhood. Aware of how Will had always struggled at school, David knew it would never be anything academic. A caring brother, he listened to Will sympathetically and with an open mind. Since their father's death and with his estate soon to be settled, Will wondered whether funds might be allocated to him, so he could buy the Hendersons' devastated property, Amaru. Surprised and curious, David asked why on earth he would want that fire-ravaged station? And what would he do there? A passionate animal lover, and a superb horseman, Will said that in addition to sheep he would love to create a horse stud. North and south of the river there was an ongoing demand for horses, ranging from Clydesdales, carriage horses, and even racehorses. Breeding ponies, Will confided, would be the best thing he ever could do. Extended family would be nearby and, in addition, Amaru was adjacent to Mirrimbali, their childhood home.

David agreed, in essence, with everything Will said, except finishing school this year. A horse stud at Amaru might be a good career choice for his brother. He certainly had demonstrated an expert way of handling that wild stallion. The river location, when cleaned up, possibly would be an excellent long-term investment, but leaving school at 16 was an issue. Sharing concern that his brother was too young and inexperienced to undertake such a project, David said, *'But you must finish school, Will, there is still so much to be learned.' 'No,'* his brother replied, *'I don't want to, especially if you are not there. I will complete this year, but that's all.'* Will then said, *'That's why Rich rode across with me. He knows I want to live on the Murray. Since the bushfire, I'm sure Amaru could be acquired very reasonably. Our cousins are nearby and I would be on the river, where we grew up. We know the land and it's a desirable location, but now completely ravaged, few farmers would want it. Rich and I both agreed it would be ideal for me. It felt like home, and it's exactly where I would love to live. I really want to create a horse stud. Trains are great, but they can only travel where rails are laid, while a horse can take you anywhere.'*

David listened in disbelief. Will was 16, but passion for his future life came through loud and clear. He was young, not scholastic, but everything he said actually made sense. The purchase of Amaru, despite its present condition was astute and would be a sound long-term asset. What Uncle John and Uncle Tam might think remained to be seen. Having been listened to without judgement by Will, David in turn responded positively, believing his brother's proposal was wise. His concern regarding Will's incomplete education was gently included. Adamantly Will insisted enough was enough. He would not return to school next year, especially without his brother.

Sylvie woke up and climbed across to enjoy the view from the window seat. With more space, David stretched out, then lay down, closing his eyes as he contemplated Will's unexpected but thought-provoking proposition. What would his brother's long-term future be in the city? Such a concept was non-existent! He was a country boy in every fibre of his being, so there was only one destination for Will, the Murray River. This school year would be completed, but nothing more. That decision was emphatic. A significant amount of time might be involved in the acquisition of Amaru, to say nothing of clearing the present carnage and then constructing a homestead, shed and yards. This timespan, most likely, would enable Will to complete another school year, but regrettably David knew his brother would never agree. If and when their father's estate did acquire this river frontage, there was no question that Will would be on site instantly, camping, or staying with nearby relatives, as he passionately involved himself in the reconstruction of Jack Henderson's former station. This project encapsulated Will's talents and his future.

David also worried about Will being so far away and living alone. Always he had been nearby to protect him. But quietly contemplating their respective lives, several realities became apparent. While his brother was only 16, it was abundantly clear that Will was passionate about his future on the Murray River. There was no alternative. In contrast, David was still vacillating regarding his career. As for living alone, Grandy possibly, would love to join his grandson. Alistair's physical contribution these days was minimal, but he had a lifetime of knowledge and experience regarding that exact land and, especially since Jane's death, he was keen to support his children and grandchildren. Even one of the McLeay cousins might like to stay with Will, and work for him. It was, after all, a short ride to Oakbank and a bit further to Argyll. Thanks to their father's estate, funds were available to pay either employees or family. Despite their wealthy home environment, both brothers had learned to be frugal. Time spent with Uncle Tam had been influential, while observation of Lady Audrey's extravagance, left them shocked. Her entire world revolved around money. Seeing what you don't want in life was just as important as seeing what you do and the brothers jointly had observed that. A workman and his wife, who could be paid to cook and manage the homestead, was another option. Initially David had been shocked at Will's proposal, but this contemplative time, stretched across the seat on the returning train, had given him time to consider everything. It actually seemed like a unique opportunity for his brother, and Amaru would be a good long-term investment. River frontage was becoming far less accessible than in their grandparents' day. Despite his initial concern, David could not think of any lifestyle better suited to his brother than beside the Murray River.

After several hours the country scenery gradually gave way to views of small farms, then houses, factories and distant church steeples. A train rattled past in the opposite direction, before their locomotive slackened pace and they arrived at the City Station. David approached a carriage driver, who agreed to transport them to Elwood. What a wonderful holiday it had been!

During Easter, the Wallace's home had been quiet and peaceful, enabling them to recharge, refresh and renew themselves after months of upheaval, yet somehow their home did not feel the same. It was lacking the vibrancy of their special trio. Cases were unpacked and then, while enjoying cool drinks before dinner, details of their holiday, including the terrifying bushfire, were relayed. *'Tam wished you had been there when Clive Henderson died, Uncle John,'* David shared. *'Everyone was shattered, but they could do nothing to help him. It was the worst few days.' 'Reading about it in the newspaper was bad enough!'* commented Aunt Cissy. *'Thank God you all survived, and we're so glad to have you safely back here.'* Both boys shared specific details about the fire and the bravery of their uncle, cousins and Grandy. It so easily could have been an annihilation, as had happened at Amaru. Will said that although they didn't have hoses, the river was an invaluable source, as well as Uncle Tam's dam between the homestead and the shed, a feature which the Hendersons' station lacked. With school in the morning and tired after their Easter holiday, Sylvie and the boys went to bed soon after dinner.

Mounted on their bicycles, with books and lunch in schoolbags, David and William waved goodbye to their sister, who shortly would walk with Cissy to her primary school. Students were enamoured listening to the Scott brothers describe terrifying hours fighting the bushfire. Some had read about the Henderson family deaths in the *Weekly Times*. They could not believe that David had visited the scene, where he actually witnessed the carnage, including the family's charred remains. It was unbelievable. The brothers shared relief that their cousins and their station had survived, but during the actual inferno, nothing could be certain from one minute to the next. Some boarders had witnessed bushfires, but for city boys it was an extraordinary account, especially hearing it first-hand.

Keen to be accepted into the University of Melbourne's School of Medicine, David worked very hard for the remainder of the year. Acknowledging that this also would be his last year, Will applied himself as best he could. However, in agreement with David, he chose to tell neither his teachers nor classmates of his decision to leave school after the final term.

Soon after they returned from the Murray, Cissy received an interesting letter from Uncle Duncan. His wife, Jess, whose cousin lived in Sydney, had written to say that locals were abuzz with gossip. Apparently Lady Audrey Parker had met and married a wealthy English nobleman. The likelihood of her ever returning to the southern continent was, it seemed, improbable. After dinner, Cissy gave David her letter. He shared the contents with Sylvie before passing it on to William. Minimal emotions were displayed. Eventually Will expressed his sentiments, *'Good luck, Lady Audrey, and all the best!'* No other reference to their stepmother was ever heard.

David's end of year results brought much joy. Having worked diligently, he was accepted into the Melbourne University's School of Medicine. Everyone was so happy for him. Uncle John and Aunt Cissy had, albeit with reluctance, agreed that Will also, would finish school. John and Cissy would have preferred their nephew to complete his education like his brother, but they knew it would involve ongoing stress. William was loved, valued and understood just as he was. Viewing school reports, John comprehended that study was difficult and taxing for his nephew. That did not mean Will wasn't talented. Gravitating to what you enjoy in life is a much wiser choice than being pressured down a path you don't like, especially when the motive is to achieve status and success. David observed one father demonstrate such pressure. The tension and stress it placed on his son was unacceptable. Eventually it took a toll on the boy's mental health.

After the Scott brothers returned from the Easter holidays at Oakbank, William asked Uncle John, executor of his father's estate, about the possibility of buying the Hendersons' ravaged station. David quietly sat in the background, listening to the discussion. Will expressed virtually everything he had shared with his brother on their return train trip. Knowing Will's talents, as well as his weaknesses, especially with study, to say nothing of his passion for country life, it seemed overall like a sensible investment. Cissy, sitting in the background, tacitly agreed. Tam, her brother, would be nearby to assist and advise, as well as her father, and the Sinclair cousins. Both she and John were cognisant of Will's academic struggles.

John contacted Angus' solicitor, Peter Hendrick, to establish the best way to proceed with the acquisition of Amaru. In due course, Peter communicated with Jack Henderson's solicitor, and in agreement with Cameron, the only surviving family member, a settlement was reached. Clearing the ravaged property of masses of rubble to present it in a saleable manner would be a major undertaking. Waiting for rain and green pastures, to say nothing of planting crops to replace blackened paddocks covered with burnt sheep carcases, was beyond the capability of Cameron and the family solicitor. Restoring Amaru would entail significant time and expense. So a low sale price was agreed. No other buyers appeared on the horizon. Will was ecstatic. It was as if all his dreams had come true. Ever since the day he had ridden round the property with his cousin, he had felt passionate about acquiring Amaru. Numerous ideas dwelled within him. He knew he could transform the devastated site. The overhaul, certainly, would be a challenge, and it would not be achieved overnight, but innately Will knew it could be done. Nothing appealed more. This was his dream. Amaru would be recreated, and how lucky was he to have this unique project, thanks to nature, timing and his father. Without the latter, he never would have had the resources to do it. His brother David, Uncle John and Aunt Cissy witnessed his elation. They didn't necessarily relate to, or understand it, but profound enthusiasm emanated from him. John especially was pleased. One aspect of administering Angus' estate had clearly been successful.

Cissy and John unquestionably would have lovingly cared for the Scott children, but a bequest in Angus' Will was an unexpected bonus. By reason of this, they decided to acquire a larger home. Their Elwood residence, purchased when they married, was modest and adequate for them. The Scott children loved staying there, but it was crowded. The boys slept in the spare bedroom, while Sylvie's bed comprised a small mattress in her aunt and uncle's room. With David and Sylvie now permanent residents, Cissy agreed with John that it would be sensible to use Angus' bequest to buy a larger home. What else would they do with this money?

As and when Will or any of the country cousins came to Melbourne, there now would be ample room for them to stay. This new house included more bedrooms, a study, sitting and dining room and a bathroom with a commode and large bathtub, both of which were connected to a drain which flowed into the garden. This modern feature made the home much more convenient than their old one. Beyond the garden shed, an outhouse adjoined the rear fence, with an opening to the lane, ensuring its contents were regularly emptied by the night cart. As well as being closer to the sea, a beautiful garden surrounded the house, with deciduous trees and multiple flowers. John could still walk to his practice, while Sylvie's school was not too far away. With David and Sylvie now permanently in residence, there was more space and individual privacy.

Some tennis courts built near the beach were an additional joy for David. Regularly he played with different local boys. At the weekends, he sometimes took Sylvie with him and encouraged her to play. A brick wall on the side of the Wallaces' new home was a perfect practice site. Sylvie's game improved greatly after she spent considerable time hitting a ball against the side of the house. She had a good eye and before long demonstrated talent with both backhand and forehand. David was thrilled, encouraging her when they played together on the bayside courts.

The Oakbank and Argyll cousins understood the concern of Will's loved ones regarding his decision to leave school, but knowing him, they completely understood his passion for life on the land. Another Christmas on the Murray was enjoyed with extended holidays. David and Sylvie then returned to Melbourne. David found work to occupy him and earn some money, before commencing at the University of Melbourne's School of Medicine. Sylvie returned to her local primary, joining special friends she had met there, while Will remained at Oakbank with Uncle Tam.

After discussions with Angus' solicitor, John decided

that with excellent contacts in the district, Will's uncle, Stuart Sinclair would be the best person to assist with advice involving the clearance and redevelopment of Amaru. Stuart would not be doing the work, but payment from the estate would be made for his advice regarding employment of local workers to clear, and then construct a homestead, shed and yards on Amaru. Creation of a simple garden also would be required. Living with Uncle Tam, Will was in constant liaison with Uncle Stuart regarding all facets of the project.

It was a source of comfort and relief for John, as executor, to have Stuart overseeing the Amaru project. Working at his Elwood practice, it was impossible to travel to the Murray and check the clearance, recovery and rebuilding of the station, and in addition, this was not his field of expertise. Will was vulnerable to being taken advantage of, but with Stuart on hand, he hoped all would be fine. Angus' solicitor relayed stories of shocking deceit and deception within estates.

Once the property was cleared, Stuart, after communicating with John and in conjunction with Will, engaged a local builder, who constructed a homestead, shed and horse yards. Will passionately expressed his ideas regarding allocation of sites and particularly the dam. Naturally the homestead maximised the river vista, but excavating a dam with views from the rear of the house provided another aesthetic outlook, as well as protection in the event of a bushfire. It all took time, but little by little Amaru was transformed. Three acorns, which eventually grew into beautiful oaks, were planted on the west side of the garden, as a tribute to Jack, Miriam and Clive Henderson. Stuart, with Will onside, oversaw a fine transformation of Amaru. Tam and John were very pleased. It was an excellent outcome at a minimal cost. Stuart always had worked hard and lived frugally, because throughout his life, money had been scarce.

As Duncan, Tam and their families had observed when Angus Scott came on the scene and married Lottie, money was abundant. Fortunately, neither David nor Will appeared to be reckless or extravagant. But for the hard-working country relations, the Oakbank MacLeays and the Argyll Sinclairs, it was with wonderment that they observed the speed with which the Hendersons' fire-ravaged property was cleared and rebuilt. Not many country people would ever have the resources to restore a devastated farm in the time that Amaru was rejuvenated.

In conjunction with Peter Hendrick, Angus' solicitor, John wound up his brother-in-law's estate. Milingil Station and Angus' harbourside home were sold. Amaru, on the banks of the Murray River, now belonged to William. A sum was given to David towards payment of his university education and affiliated costs. Many of his friends and acquaintances were living at Trinity College, which he also could have done, but he preferred to stay with his uncle, aunt and little sister. Sylvie's inheritance, equal to her brothers', was yet to be allotted to her. In due course it would pay for her secondary education and ongoing needs. John and Cissy were especially appreciative of the bequest Angus had left them. They loved their new home. With much more space and David and Sylvie now permanent residents, it was beneficial for everyone. All the estate transactions were meticulously recorded by John, while the balance remained in a Bank of New South Wales account.

One evening in the early 1890s as Cissy was preparing dinner, a carriage pulled up outside their Elwood home and shortly afterwards footsteps were heard, followed by a knock at the door. David was studying in his room and John, relaxing in the sitting room, was reading the newspaper after a long day at work. Sylvie was trying to complete a picture puzzle. As Cissy opened the front door, she recognised Mr Peter Hendrick, Angus Scott's solicitor. *'Good evening, Mrs Wallace, I'm sorry to trouble you, but this afternoon I received a call from Emmerson Smith, Mr Scott's accountant. Mr Smith is extremely worried about a looming financial recession. An astute businessman, who has managed Mr Scott's affairs for years, Emmerson requested that I contact Dr Wallace. Instructions are that, as executor, he must immediately withdraw as much money as he safely can from Mr Scott's estate, and stow it securely. Two major Victorian banks collapsed this morning. Mr Smith is advising all his clients to act immediately.'* What a very strange request at this hour of the night! Cissy called John who was joined by David. Listening to Mr Hendrick's repeated directive, both were shocked. This was a strange mandate, but to deliver such a definitive instruction, late in the evening, meant the accountant's advice must be critical.

John responded that first thing in the morning he would travel to the city and withdraw as much money from the Scott estate as was safely possible. His wife would accompany him. *'According to Emmerson, even tomorrow may be too late,'* Mr Hendrick said, while declining refreshments. *'I still have another client to inform.'* John in somewhat of a daze, accompanied Mr Hendrick to his carriage. The Wallaces then sat down with David, mesmerised. Cissy said she definitely would accompany John to the city bank. A note to his medical practice was written, saying that due to unforeseen circumstances, Dr Wallace would be unable to attend patients until the following day. David, also shocked and surprised, said he would take Sylvie to school and deliver his uncle's message to his medical clinic. Dinner was delayed. Instead of returning to the kitchen, Cissy remained with her husband and nephew, discussing this frightening and unprecedented situation. They all were cognisant of the estate's finances, which included David and Sylvie's inheritance. Where was money ever safer than in a bank? What unpredictable circumstances must be on the horizon?

Early the next morning the Wallaces rose, ate breakfast and walked to Ripponlea Station. Usually, this promenade towards the railway line, past picturesque homes and gardens, was a routine exercise which the couple loved, but today both pedestrians were preoccupied and agitated. Their friendly neighbour milking his cow waved, but unusually no acknowledgement was received.

A train arrived soon after they reached the station, ensuring a swift journey to the city. Together they walked along Swanston Street, turning at Collins Street and entering a very crowded bank. After a substantial wait, the manager appeared, ushering them into his office. After confirming John Wallace's identity, he agreed that money could be withdrawn from the estate of Angus Scott. In an agitated manner, the manager relayed that yesterday and this morning had been distressing and unparalleled. Observing the estate balance, it was evident to John that there was a sizeable loss. Cissy was carrying a large handbag in which to stow the currency. There was no question as to withdrawing the funds. In just 24 hours, huge losses had occurred. John withdrew the estate's remaining money. It was arranged in the manager's office, so there were no observers. Cissy asked whatever had caused this financial catastrophe, and where the missing estate funds were. Clearly distressed, the manager was unable to explain any cause. Instead, he hurried to assist other waiting customers.

Numerous clients had lost all or most of their savings. The trigger was unknown. It had been sudden and unexpected. The Wallaces shared their genuine concern and thanked the manager, before slowly pressing their way through a long queue in the densely packed foyer, to Collins Street.

Just a little further ahead was the Mutual Provident Land Investing & Building Society, where John had invested his small savings. One of his patients, a trusted friend, was a director. But upon arrival, they saw that sadly the building was closed. It proved to be yet another organisation to suffer irretrievable financial losses.

Shocked, the Wallace's sat on nearby seat, as slowly they accepted this awful reality. Then John shared that although they had lost their savings, at least he had salvaged the remaining estate funds. Grateful to have withdrawn what to most people was still a sizeable sum, they agreed that a carriage home would be safer than the train. With exhaustion and some relief, they arrived at their Elwood home, carefully carrying the currency indoors. Sylvie was at school, but David joined them in the sitting room as the morning's circumstances were shared. Importantly and first of all, they considered where the safest place to store the estate pound notes might be. They did not own a safe. The ceiling seemed a good idea, unless there was a fire. Lots of discussion took place. Perhaps a sealed container buried in the garden, or somewhere in the shed? Eventually a decision was made. In a corner of the sitting room, a manhole provided entry to a cavity between the ceiling and the roof. David carried in a ladder from the shed. Cissy emptied the pound notes from her handbag, wrapped them in a scarf, placed them in a metal box and then gave them to her nephew. David carefully mounted the ladder, climbed into the ceiling cavity and stowed away his father's remaining money.

Within days it was apparent that Victoria was in the throes of a severe financial recession. A significant amount of money had been lost from Angus Scott's estate, but compared to most people, they were fortunate. Without Emmerson Smith's prompt advice, nothing most likely would have been left. More Victorian banks collapsed as well as several in New South Wales. Ever since the Gold Rush, Victoria had flourished, but suddenly, in contrast, there was complete devastation. Innumerable people faced terrible times, losing not only their savings but their homes, and in rural areas, farms as well. It was unbelievably stressful. John felt liability for the Scott children as executor of their father's estate. Of course, the losses were not his fault, but he was, nevertheless, very anxious. That Amaru had been purchased and money dispatched to Stuart for construction of the Murray River station was so fortuitous. Like all the family, John had been hesitant about acquiescing to Will's desire for Amaru, but what a relief that he had proceeded. Thankfully the MacLeay and Sinclair families on the Murray were fine. Both had their properties, but no additional savings. This recession was unforeseen, but if the entire estate money had been lost, John would have suffered great distress. Funds had disappeared, but how much worse might it have been.

Several of John's patients were in dire straits having suffered excruciating financial losses, which never could be recovered. Significant time was spent travelling by horse and cart to attend patients with ongoing ill health, as well as responding to messages left at the practice regarding accidents. Tragically, several people, severely impacted financially and in poor health, just gave up the battle. No fees were charged where people had been left penniless. How blessed were he and Cissy to have their home, his practice, and the Scott children? The clinic's other practitioner, Dr Fredrick Black, also declined to charge patients suffering severe financial hardship, but for him it was very challenging. He, too, had suffered significant losses while endeavouring to support a large family. People everywhere were desperate. That John and Cissy had purchased their new home, rather than leave Angus' bequest in the bank, was such a blessing. Unquestionably that money would have vanished.

Chapter Nineteen

DESPITE BEING SURROUNDED BY THIS FINANCIAL upheaval, life had to go on. The Elwood household settled into a routine as best they could. Cissy nurtured their vegetable garden and orchard, while supporting struggling neighbours. John worked long hours at his practice, David travelled each day to the Melbourne University School of Medicine, while Sylvie attended her primary school. As well as practising her tennis, Sylvie worked hard with support from Cissy at playing the piano. She clearly had musical talent and received encouragement from the Elwood household. They all loved hearing her play. Regularly David shared aspects of his course with Uncle John. It was interesting and beneficial for them both.

Whenever there was a holiday break, the Scott siblings naturally travelled to the Murray to stay with their brother. It was amazing to see the transformation of Amaru and to observe Will totally absorbed in his work. Although young and inexperienced, Will had tremendous energy and was passionate about his property and especially his horses.

On advice from Stuart Sinclair, John had agreed to the employment of a manager and his wife at Amaru. For many years, Ted with his wife Mary had managed a large station on the Murrumbidgee River, but after its sudden sale, Ted was left without work. Stuart's sister, Maisie, and her husband, living on a neighbouring run, advised Stuart of their predicament. With neither home nor income, Ted and Mary gratefully accepted employment at Amaru. Ted was 50 but he had extensive knowledge and experience with sheep, while his wife, Mary, was more than happy to cook and manage the homestead. It proved to be an agreeable and successful arrangement for several years. Will learned so much from Ted, while the older manager valued Will's youthful energy and enthusiasm. Both were relaxed, grounded and loved life on the land. Each morning Will milked their dairy cow, before delivering the pail to Mary who scalded it in preparation for drinking.

After the homestead was built and before Ted's arrival, Grandy stayed with Will at Amaru and much was learned from his grandfather's extensive knowledge of the river-land. Aunty Grace regularly provided food for Will, who otherwise managed himself. Grandy's stay proved to be an emotional and special bonding time. In the evening beside the fire, as well as outdoors, Alistair shared with his grandson stories of his early life in Scotland, his elopement with Jane and their challenging life on the Murray in the 1850's. Since he had lost his mother at a young age, these family chronicles for

Will were precious. Listening to his grandfather reminisce about his dearly loved children, Sandy and Lottie, both of whom left this world too soon, multiple memories of his mother resurfaced for Will. Since his mother's death, no one ever held or hugged him as she had. David was his enduring stalwart, but he also, had been deprived of his mother's loving caresses. Of course, they had the caring support of Aunty Cissy's and Uncle Tam's families, but it wasn't the same as Mother. These reminiscences prompted him also to think of his little sister. Sylvie was loved by her aunt and uncle as their own child, but she had never known her mother. Thinking how much he missed those maternal hugs, Will decided that from now on, every time he saw his little sister, he would hug her and tell her he loved her. Grandy always said, *'Love is not for us to keep, love is to give away.'*

One evening, sitting with Grandy beside the fireplace, Will was conscious of occasional tears trickling down his face as stories were shared. He had never grieved openly. But suddenly in the forefront of his mind was that day when the 13 and 11-year-old brothers were summoned to their headmaster's office and told of their mother's death. It was a case of *'I'm sorry, boys, but sadly your mother has died. Now chin up, and please pack your cases. I will arrange transport to the station, for a train ride home.'* Clearly there was no such thing as grief. Then, on arrival at Mirrimbali, their father, Angus, engulfed in shock and distress, lacked the capacity to support his sons. Minimal love or sympathy was given to the boys at this vulnerable time. Barely had their mother been buried before they were transported to their father's property west of Sydney, where a governess and maid cared for them. It seemed like, '*This is life. Just accept it, and get over it!*' A year later, they were sent to boarding school in Sydney. When father died it had been different. Dear Cissy and Uncle John had travelled to Sydney with Sylvie to support them. They had been surrounded by love, sympathy and understanding.

Will especially loved Grandy's stories of his childhood in the Scottish Highlands. Freezing winters where snow covered the entire countryside sounded fascinating. Will never had seen snow. Alistair's love for his Scottish parents and brother also was expressed. It was a great sorrow that he never had seen them again. '*If only Jane's father had allowed us to marry, that never would have happened.*' After which he quietly reminisced, '*But then look at my wonderful family here. Struggling with and conquering life's challenges strengthens us and sometimes reveals unexpected and enriching experiences. Your darling grandmother always demonstrated this.*' Will had no idea that his grandparents were forced to leave their homeland because Granny Jane was forbidden to marry Grandy. It sounded very harsh. How brave were they, to trek across the Highlands and survive terrifying storms at sea. Grandy's brother, Archie, still in the Highlands, apparently had been a loyal and wonderful correspondent.

Over the years, Will and his brother had spent considerable

time with Grandy, both at Uncle Tam's and Aunt Cissy's, but never had Will heard him share in this extensive and heartfelt manner. Maybe Will was too young to remember, or possibly times were too busy with children and grandchildren. Dear Grandy, like his darling Jane, never was self-centred. If unable to help, he remained unobtrusively in the background. Presumably this time at Amaru, with nothing else to do in the evenings and memories of his settlement here in the 1850's after the stress of their elopement, had triggered his memory. Will valued everything his grandfather shared. It almost seemed as if some emptiness within had been filled. Sharing and listening had been a treasured exchange for both.

The next evening as they sat beside the fire, Will asked, *'Please, Grandy, tell me more about your life. I loved everything I heard last night.'* Alistair's next narrative, beside the burning hearth, described the amazing surprise and unbelievable joy his darling Jane experienced when her dearly loved brother, whom she had not seen for 10 years, unexpectedly turned up on their doorstep. It was extraordinary. Duncan had travelled all the way from Scotland. Then, just a few years later, Hunter, her older brother, with his family, sailed across the Pacific Ocean from Philadelphia to find his younger siblings. Both visits had meant so much to Jane. Will recalled vaguely hearing these tales as a child, but never could they be compared to Grandy's emotional descriptions of them. Campbell Sinclair, Uncle Stuart's brother, so loved meeting

213

his American cousins that he had travelled to Philadelphia and stayed with Hunter's family. If Will had met Campbell, he must have been a child, because he could not remember him. *'Well, he now lives in Perth,'* Grandy said. *'When Campbell went to America, Uncle Duncan and Aunty Jess were concerned that he would not return. He loved his time there, but luckily he came back, living in Sydney for a while, before moving to Perth. But unfortunately, it's so far across the Nullarbor Plain to Western Australia that neither Maisie, Stuart, nor his parents have seen him since.'* Whether any of these faraway relations ever would be seen again was a curiosity. Will knew he would love to meet them. And although he loved the Murray River, where all his family had lived, listening to his grandfather made him think that one day he would love to explore the world beyond his fast-flowing stream.

After Ted and Mary arrived at Amaru, Alistair reverted back to his routine of staying in turn with his son Tam on the Murray and his daughter Cissy in the city. It was a lovely combination. Melbourne visits gave him time to catch up with David, studying at university, and Sylvie, at primary school, as well as his regular walks to the beach. In contrast, life at Oakbank was busier. Robert now ran the station with his father, which was invaluable to Tam. Sheep, cattle and diverse crops flourished. Richard MacLeay, the older brother, had taken a job on a station in north western New South Wales. It seemed very remote, but letters home indicated he was loving it. Rose attended the local school to which she rode each day with her friend Elsie, who's family lived on the northern side of the road en route to the township. Elsie's farm was expansive, but there was, of course, no river access, so on hot summer days Elise and her brothers often rode over to Oakbank to cool down and enjoy a refreshing swim. Even though Alistair could no longer do much physically, just standing on the road to block the herd, or helping at the yards, or at shearing time, was useful. Unlike other workers, he instinctively knew what was required. Time with Will at Amaru was greatly valued and he knew how much he helped his grandson. It seemed that his manager Ted principally oversaw the sheep, while Will was occupied with breeding and training his horses.

Will, guided by Ted, learned so much. The number of sheep was sizeable, ensuring constant maintenance. Shearing, dipping and breeding were continuous, according to the season. Thankfully, with his father's inheritance, Amaru like Mirrimbali had been fenced off, so that Will on horseback with his dogs moved the flock to respective paddocks as the pasture was eaten down. He also ploughed up acres, dragging the dray behind his draught horses, so that crops could be planted. And in spite of his busy work schedule, Will was in regular contact with Uncle Tam and Robert nearby, as well as his second cousins, the Sinclairs, at Argyll. Having grown up together, they felt like one large family.

After a fine stallion was acquired from a breeder near

Albury, Will's mares duly delivered some sturdy young ponies, which he enthusiastically trained in the yards. Horses were in great demand. More and more land was being settled, and one of the most important requirements on any station was horses. Picnic race meetings became popular events, both north and south of the river. Young local men competed in these events riding their fleetest ponies. Each race meeting usually was followed by a black tie ball in the evening. Soon they became a wonderful form of community entertainment in the country. Not only older residents rekindled friendships at these get-togethers, but they were especially good for the younger generation. Life on remote stations was challenging with minimal social interaction, so picnic races followed by evening balls, became an ideal way for young men to ride their ponies in competitions and interact with ladies, often farmers' daughters and sometimes city friends, who had been invited for the occasion. People travelled vast distances to enjoy these rural festivities. They added a special dimension to country life, especially for the young.

Before long, one horse and his jockey were becoming household names at picnic race meetings in the Riverina. Most of the participants bred and rode their own steeds, but not many could compete with William Scott and Stardust. Wherever they raced, few horses and riders ever eclipsed them. One year they were particularly successful. By reason of this, Amaru horses suddenly were in great demand, and

216

not just reliable workhorses. Racing enthusiasts, including city dwellers, sought to acquire steeds bred and trained on this Murray River stud.

Will was only doing what he loved best, following his passion, but as a consequence, his stud was becoming financially viable. Success and notoriety were to him not just inconsequential, but distasteful. He adored riding with Stardust, but publicity in the local press did not appeal. It was therefore with considerable surprise that he received a letter asking if he would agree to enter Stardust in this year's Melbourne Cup. A guest at the Deniliquin Picnic Races, Edmund Brown, who witnessed Will's winning ride, wrote that he would very much like to nominate Stardust and Will. Transport via train to the city could be arranged and stables on a farm near Flemington were available. Will was apprehensive. How would his dearly loved stallion cope on a train? It possibly would be traumatic for him. Will did not think he wanted to go to Melbourne, or participate in a city race. He loved country life, as did Stardust.

In due course Will's extended family became aware of this invitation, and despite his reluctance, both the city and country families were keen for him to acquiesce. Grandy, Uncle Tam, Aunty Grace and their family said they would definitely come to this year's Melbourne Cup if Will rode Stardust. The Argyll Sinclairs also were enthusiastic, while his brother and sister with Aunt Cissy and Uncle John naturally would be present. Will vacillated. He was not sure he wanted to do this. Publicity he had received in the country was quite enough. If there was one thing he never liked, it was being the centre of attention. In a few months, the Melbourne Cup would be run, on the first Tuesday in November. Will decided not to participate as the prospect was causing him disquiet.

Then, unexpectedly, without notice, David arrived at Amaru. Throughout his life, no one had been more supportive than his brother. What a welcome surprise! Will loved living on the banks of the Murray, but the one thing he did miss, especially in situations like the present, was access to his brother. Just someone understanding and non-judgemental to talk to, was invaluable. How often he would have loved David to be nearby. Of course, he could write to him, but it wasn't the same.

Initially time was spent inspecting the property, during which Will disclosed what was being done and what was proposed. For David, life here would be daunting. These were challenges with which he never could cope and would never wish to. But for Will it was the reverse. Amaru was his world. There was, of course, no pressure from his city brother. Eventually, while down at the horse yards, the prospect of the Melbourne Cup was aired. Will expressed his apprehension. It wasn't the actual ride; in fact, that didn't worry him at all. His special passion with Stardust was racing. He loved it. But the attention and publicity, especially in the city, did not appeal.

David agreed. He, too, was happy to live his life in privacy, outside the press. He reiterated to Will that whatever was right for him, was what mattered. They walked back to the homestead. David shared that if Will did decide to ride in the Melbourne Cup, then he would come to Amaru and accompany him with Stardust on the train. He also pointed out that, at the end of the day, it was just a race, on just one day. After all, how important was it? Could Will remember the name of anyone who rode in last year's Melbourne Cup? Of course, he couldn't. David also gently pointed out that, unlike for other riders, for Will there was no pressure. *'All our family know that you don't care whether you win or lose. If you and Stardust enjoy the race, that's all that matters. And that's how we all feel. But I believe it would be a special experience for you. How many people, ever, would be invited to compete! Will, you always have been such a talented rider! I never could do it, nor could anyone I know. It would give your family such joy to watch you and Stardust and we don't care about the result. As long as you enjoy the ride, that's all that matters.'*

As so often was the case, Will felt one hundred times better after confiding in his brother. How true! That's all it was, just a race. Instead of thinking of himself, Will began to think of Cissy and Uncle John, his neighbouring cousins and that if he and Stardust did compete, it might be a fun and truly memorable day for all his family. He walked over to David, gave him a hug and said, *'Yes, my brother, thanks to you, Stardust and I will race!'*

David stayed a few more days before returning to the city. Ted and Mary especially enjoyed his time at Amaru. He couldn't contribute on the station in the manner Will did, but his positive influence on his brother was clearly evident. Will was so much more confident. Ted and Mary never had attended a Melbourne Cup, nor visited Melbourne, but they certainly were aware of the race's popularity. Hearing that Will had agreed to compete with Stardust gave them so much pleasure. Everyone throughout their entire life rode horses, but Ted never had seen a rider like Will. Regardless of which horse he rode, it was as if he and the mount were one.

David said that, through contacts, he would make enquiries about Edmund Brown. Access to stables and a paddock near the racecourse at Flemington seemed sensible. It was a long way from Elwood where Will would be staying, but hopefully Stardust would be well cared for. *'Will, there's a train at Ripponlea, not far from Aunt Cissy's new home, which takes you into the city and then you can catch another one to Flemington. If this man wants you to compete, I'm sure it will be in his interest to take good care of Stardust.'* Will agreed. Trains had made a huge difference to travel. Will harnessed his mare and drove David to the local station and farewelled him. The Amaru orchard and vegetable garden were flourishing, but a trip to the township always was useful, so Mary asked Will to purchase one or two items while there. It was sad waving goodbye to his brother, but how special that he had come.

If only he lived closer, Will mused, but of course both were following their respective paths.

As he drove his cart home, Will felt much more lighthearted than prior to David's visit. Competing in the upcoming Melbourne Cup would be quite an experience. It was still weeks away, so why worry about it. *'Just keep the focus on today and what I need to achieve here and now,'* he reflected. The outcome was beyond his control, so as David had said, *'Why not just enjoy it, and do the best you can.'* Trotting along in the cart, he commenced singing. What a lovely spring day it was and how blessed he was, with life here on the Murray.

Each day Will rode Stardust round the property, engaging him in lengthy sprints. Stock was moved and other chores were met. Then, six weeks later, David returned. Edmund Brown, according to contacts, was well regarded in the racing industry. With his trainer, he would meet their locomotive tomorrow at a northern station and lead Stardust to stables on the nearby farm. Equipment for the racing stallion, as well as Will's own needs, was packed and loaded onto the cart. Ted drove David to the local station, while Will followed on Stardust. With reluctance, Stardust was herded into a livestock carriage at the rear, after which the boys stepped on board and the train set off.

Will was anxious for Stardust, but nothing could be done throughout the duration of their trip. When eventually the train stopped at the northern city station, Edmund Brown, as arranged, was waiting on the platform along with his trainer. Will and David alighted with their luggage. Will focused on his steed, while David took their baggage to the ticket office, asking if it might be stowed there. Slowly and gently Stardust was encouraged out of his carriage. Satisfied that his equestrian passenger had been safely unloaded, the train driver gave his 'all clear signal', sounded the whistle and then continued on to Central Station. Will did not want to abandon his stallion, but Edmund Brown assured him that Stardust would be carefully handled. The journey clearly had unnerved Stardust as he was flighty and unstable. A drink was proffered, after which the trainer led him through an opening at the rear of the platform. The boys then watched as the trainer placed a saddle on Stardust, mounted him and followed Edmund Brown in his carriage. Anxious about his stallion, Will said he would come to the farm tomorrow. It was positioned just over a mile from the Flemington Station, so it would not be too far to walk. Edmund said that their entry in the Cup had been confirmed.

Since there was a long wait before the next train, David and Will collected their luggage and hired a carriage to the City Station from where they caught another train to Ripponlea. Will expressed his concern about Stardust, but David was sure he would be fine. His wellbeing, after all, was in Edmund Brown's interests. A short walk from Ripponlea took them to the Wallaces' new home, more spacious than the old residence with which Will was familiar. Sylvie was so happy to have David home again, and added to that was the joy of her dear country brother. After his recent emotional conversations with Grandy, Will gave Sylvie a hug and told her that he loved her, just as his mother always had done with him. How Sylvie felt about it, he didn't know, but he was happy.

It was Friday evening, so just the weekend and Monday lay ahead before Will and Stardust would hit the track. Excitedly, Sylvie relayed that she had told her school friend Mollie that her brother was riding Stardust in the Melbourne Cup. Mollie's parents always attended this annual race meeting. Her father especially loved the event. Usually Mollie stayed with her grandmother, but her parents agreed that if Sylvie's brother was a competitor in the big race this year, she would accompany them. At school this morning, Mollie had been so excited. Will said he didn't have any expectations. Never before had he ridden in the city, so he planned to just enjoy the event. Unlike at smaller country race meetings, he didn't think Stardust could outride all the Melbourne rivals.

The Wallaces believed Sylvie was too young to attend the race, but with Mollie going, and Will competing in this special Melbourne Cup, the decision was made to take her. They would go via train, arriving well before the Cup, but they would not stay for later events.

Sylvie's best dress, bonnet and shoes were selected. Cissy, too, chose a stylish frock with a matching hat and gloves, while John's three-piece tweed suit and top hat were laid out in readiness. Everyone was looking forward to Tuesday. On Monday, Grandy, Uncle Tam, Aunty Grace, Robert and Rose came to Melbourne on the train. Uncle Duncan and Cowgirl Jess, as she still was called, decided not to come, but their son Stuart, who had been so helpful to Will, caught the train with the MacLeays. It was a long time since the country cousins had visited the city. Grandy, Uncle Tam and Aunty Grace stayed at Elwood while Rose shared Sylvie's room. David and Will pitched a tent in the lovely garden which they shared with cousin Robert. Uncle Stuart stayed with friends. Thankfully the weather was mild.

Each morning on Saturday, Sunday and Monday, Will caught a train to the city, then another across to Flemington to check Stardust. Out of his natural environment, the stallion seemed a little agitated, but Will endeavoured to soothe and pacify him, just taking him for quiet rides around the neighbourhood. Details regarding the horse and jockey had been provided to Edmund Brown for submission to the racing officials. Finally, Tuesday came and after enjoying Cissy's early breakfast, the Scott brothers, with cousin Robert, set off for the Flemington stables. David was agreeably pleased that, in spite of the day ahead, Will seemed calm and relaxed. Deep within himself Will knew that without the presence of his brother, he never would be undertaking this challenge. Thinking of the day ahead, his father, Angus, a gifted rider, came to mind, as well as his beautiful mother. Memories of their love and patience, teaching him to swim and ride beside the Murray, were at the forefront of his mind. Today he would race for them.

Alighting at the Flemington Station, the boys walked to the small farm where Stardust was stabled. Edmund Brown and his trainer greeted them. Stardust had been fed and groomed, but still seemed a little agitated. Will's presence was effective. He stroked and soothed his dearly loved horse, calming him. The racecourse was just a short distance away. After saddling Stardust, Will and Edmund's trainer rode across to the Melbourne Cup track. Unfamiliar with the procedure, Will quietly followed his accomplice. Stardust was identified, after which they were directed to his allocated stall.

Back at the Flemington farm, Edmund Brown offered the boys a lift to the racecourse in his carriage, but thanking him, David and Robert chose to walk. Mid-morning on the first Tuesday in November, Flemington Racecourse was hectic. Innumerable horses were entering and awaiting direction. This environment was the reverse to Amaru, but Will continued to pacify Stardust, as they settled into their allocated stall which was a long way down, at the end of the mounting yards. After walking back from the farm, David and Robert eventually found them. Viewing contestants, as they walked the length of the mounting yards, the cousins expressed joint reservations as to Stardust's chance of winning. Never had they seen so many prize horses. Will told the boys that four steeds had come by ship from Sydney and another from New Zealand. This event was certainly unique. Country race meetings, casual and relaxed, were definitely not in this class.

After the early departure of the boys, the Elwood home was less crowded but still busy. Grace helped Cissy pack two large picnic baskets, while John fitted large rugs into a carry bag. The day was sunny with no sign of rain. Rather than walk to the station carrying picnic gear, and wait for trains, Tam arranged for a carriage to collect all seven excited spectators and transport them to Flemington Racecourse. It was earlier than planned, but they set off anyway, arriving in time to find a perfect picnic spot, just near the finishing post. After settling in, Uncle John set off to the mounting yards, with a view to find the boys, so that all the family could enjoy lunch together. Cissy was very pleased they left when they did as crowds were pouring in. Their position near the finishing post was perfect, but had they come later, this location would not have been available.

Walking past the long line of stalls, Dr John, like David and Robert, now understood why Will had no expectation of victory. Finely bred horses receiving first class attention lined the walk. Eventually, at the rear, he found Stardust. David and Robert were sitting up on the rails watching Will groom his stallion. Shortly after, Uncle Stuart, who had come on the train, found them. Having no idea where Will's family might be, he decided that finding Stardust would be his best hope. Uncle John requested they all come now to enjoy an early picnic lunch on the grass. Everyone agreed except Will. He didn't want to leave Stardust. But his brother pointed out that it was very important that he ate some food before the race. Edmund Brown's trainer was due back any minute. Stuart spoke up. He agreed that Will needed to be nourished, and said he would remain in the stall with Stardust until Will returned. John told him where their picnic site was, literally in front of the finishing post. Stuart was certain he would find them and reassured Will that he would remain with Stardust until he returned. *'You won't have to find our family, Uncle Stuart, because I will definitely return with Will,'* David told him, *'and then we can go back to our picnic spot together.'*

It was a warm day with Spring sunshine and no wind. Uncle John led them to the ideal position they had selected adjacent to the finishing post. Crowds were arriving, with everyone looking for suitable locations to view the race. Ladies stepped out in stylish attire, while gentlemen wore tailored suits and top hats. Delicious chicken sandwiches were enjoyed, followed by beautiful cakes. It certainly was a happy and memorable picnic. Tam carried across a wooden chair he found for his father, as everyone else spread out on the rug. If only Jane were here, Alistair thought, as he lovingly watched his son, daughter and extended family.

Unsurprisingly, Will seemed a little tense. *'I have placed bets on Stardust, Will,'* Tam said, *'so we're hopeful of a win.'* Will replied that he valued his uncle's faith in his stallion, but after seeing some of the contestants, he was not confident.

'There are horses in the stables, the like of which I've never seen,' he said. *'Amazing breeds. I don't think Stardust will stand much of a chance against several of them. Also, there are 32 horses in the race. Never have we ridden with so many competitors.'* Will savoured his aunt's sandwiches, as well as a drink and delicious chocolate cake, before saying it was time to return to Stardust. Emotionally moved by the scene before him, he went first to his grandfather, then his mother's siblings, Uncle Tam and Aunt Cissy, hugging them lovingly. It was not just their support today, but years of generosity, guidance and life values. Things which one can't buy. *'Good luck, Will!'* was reiterated by all. *'We're with you, and our fingers are crossed,'* echoed in his ears as he walked away. David signalled goodbye as well, following his brother. He had promised his little sister that when he returned, before Will's race commenced, he would lift her onto his shoulders, ensuring she had a perfect view. Sylvie couldn't wait!

There were just two more races, then the Melbourne Cup. All the food was eaten, drinks finished and cups and plates were stowed back in the picnic baskets. Cissy nevertheless set aside a small package for Stuart, who was minding Stardust. Tam remarked that although it would be a long time standing, getting the best viewing positions now would be wise, especially with this large crowd. Everyone agreed and settled along the rail, almost opposite the finishing post. Earlier, with Rose, Sylvie had wandered off in search of Mollie, but attendance was so vast that they had no hope of finding her school friend. Waiting by the track, Grace shared that last year her cousin had come to the Cup, but it had poured with rain. The entire course had been drenched. It had been a disappointing day with few in attendance. How lucky were they today? The weather was perfect.

The race before the Cup came and went swiftly. David returned, revealing that Will and Stardust had left the stables and shortly would enter the track. Uncle Stuart, who had remained with Stardust in his stall, came also and was most appreciative of the snack Cissy had saved for him. As Stuart greeted everyone, he expressed disbelief at their perfect position, right beside the finishing post! Leaning across the rail and peering into the distance, David said that he could see horses and riders assembling at the starting point. Everyone stretched over the rail straining to see Stardust. Excitement was at fever pitch!

Not long afterwards, at 3 o'clock, a loud bang was heard and the race commenced. Hurtling up the track towards them came the horses. Hooves were flying, but with 32 chargers, Will's eager family struggled to find him. *'There he is, in the middle,'* yelled David, *'he's wearing a navy cap.'* Sitting on David's shoulders, Sylvie excitedly cheered Will. In a flash of flying hooves and cracking whips, they sped past the finishing post, racing round the bend, with one more lap to complete. Across the field, the crowd followed a dense moving mass, with flying hooves leaving a trail of dust. But as to exactly where Stardust and Will were, no one could determine. As the sprint continued round the field in the distance, Will's devoted spectators were glued to the horses speeding along the track. Flying hooves approached the bend as they raced into the final strait. *'Go, Will, go!'* cried Sylvie.

A grey mare broke away leaving the others in her wake. Huge excitement now set in amongst the entire crowd. In the grandstand, spectators previously seated were on their feet, cheering. Will's family leant across the rail. Where was Stardust? The grey mare held her lead. Then, just as they were giving up hope, who should break away from the pack, hurtling down the strait at breakneck speed towards the frontrunner, but a black stallion. It was their champion! *'Go, Will! Go Stardust!'* was the unified cry. Even lots of surrounding people were cheering Stardust. With unbelievable speed and determination, Stardust overtook the grey mare. This was extraordinary, beyond the family's belief! The tension was palpable. Whips were cracking, as flying steeds bore down on the two frontrunners. Will urged Stardust on, but thundering hooves were on their trail. Another horse had passed the mare and came up beside him. The two leaders were neck and neck! As the horses approached the finishing post, the crowd was euphoric, jumping for joy. What a contest. *'Go, Stardust, go!'* they yelled. But just as Stardust reached the winning post, so did Fighter. With incredible speed, Fighter hit the front and passed Stardust by half a head. This was a race like no other. Stardust had broken the record for the Melbourne Cup, but so had another horse,

Fighter, by half a head. Today's race was one of the most memorable Melbourne Cups ever ridden. The crowd was ecstatic, clapping, cheering and shouting.

Will trotted over to Fighter, heartily congratulating his rider. What a race it had been! Herbert, Fighter's jockey, reciprocated with genuine admiration saying, *'How we got there, I do not know. You seemed so far ahead.'* Suddenly photographers and other people surrounded Fighter, which gave Will an opportunity to slip into the background. He started heading back to Stardust's stall, but en route he was circumvented and directed to the presentation centre. He may not have been the winner, but after such a race there was more than acknowledgement for today's second place. With reluctance, Will followed. Trotting along, he remembered his brother's words. *'It's just one day, Will, it's just a race. In other words, enjoy it!'* Well, why not, he thought, knowing his parents would have been very proud of him, to say nothing of all his family here today.

A speech was made and Herbert was presented with the Melbourne Cup. A local boy, Herbert accepted his prize with much joy, thanking his family and praising his brave winner, Fighter. He also acknowledged Stardust and Will and the grey mare, Sapphire, admitting that he never thought Fighter could overtake them. The Cup record had been broken by two horses, Stardust and Fighter. This was the fastest Melbourne Cup ever ridden. Will was grateful that he was not required to speak, but what a day it had been. His family was overjoyed. After lots of hugs and congratulations for their champion, Will's grandfather, Cissy, John, Tam, Grace and the girls returned to Elwood by carriage. Uncle Stuart, also very thrilled that he had travelled down from Argyll, hugged Will. His parents, Duncan and Jess, had been unable to attend, and he so regretted they had not witnessed this remarkable ride.

Edmund Brown, waiting at Stardust's stall, was equally over the moon. After sharing their joy at Will's ride, Robert and David walked back to the Flemington farm, with Will mounted on Stardust ambling beside them. It was a first Melbourne Cup for all of them, but never could they expect to attend another like this. Stardust was settled into stables at the nearby farm after which the boys walked back towards the station. Discussing this truly extraordinary day, they strolled along the road for quite some distance, before David sighted a carriage and signalled the driver, who drove them to a popular pub in the city. A few well-earned celebratory drinks were enjoyed before the boys caught the train back to Elwood. It was such a happy and memorable night. The pub was packed with lots of racegoers celebrating the Cup. Seated at a corner table with his brother and cousin, Will was very happy to be unrecognised. Walking to the station, David remarked, *'I think those few drinks will be beneficial for a good night's sleep in our tent, although, Will, I'm sure you'll go out like a light, after your ride!'* Will laughed. For him, it had been more than a ride. It was a life lesson. Face fear and go for it! Never, without the encouragement of his brother, would he have entered the Melbourne Cup. Stardust had been remarkable. He loved the ride, and for his family it had been an unforgettable day.

The next morning, after goodbye hugs and many thanks, Will left early for the Flemington stables via the connecting trains. He then walked to the nearby small farm to collect his prize stallion. Edmund's trainer, on horseback, accompanied Will, as he rode Stardust to the northern station. Arrangements had been made for a livestock carriage to be attached to today's Murray River train. They waited some time until it eventually arrived. Having caught the locomotive in the city, Uncle Tam, Aunty Grace, Robert and Rose were on board. Watching out the window for his cousin, Robert leapt down to help Will entice Stardust into the rear horse carriage. Time spent on a train did not appeal to Stardust, but eventually they managed to secure him safely on board. Advised that his equestrian passenger was the horse that broke the record at yesterday's Melbourne Cup, the driver stepped down from his cabin to view this celebrated champion. After watching the successful boarding process, he approached Will, shaking hands and congratulating him on his Melbourne Cup win. Will responded that it had been a great race, but regrettably Stardust was the runner up, not the winner. Pleased, nevertheless, to be transporting such passengers, the train driver cheerily stepped back into his cabin and sounded the whistle, as they set off for the Murray

River. Will joined his cousins in their carriage. Everyone was still on a high after yesterday's race.

Although Will would miss David, Sylvie and his uncle and aunt, arriving home at Amaru felt so good. For some people, life, after breaking a record at the Melbourne Cup, might seem a bit of a letdown, but not for Will. Awake with the sparrows the following morning, he was out on the property, working with his horses and moving sheep under directions from Ted. There was so much to be done. Just a few weeks away, Christmas this year would be special. David and Sylvie were coming to stay and planned to remain at Amaru for most of January. Grandy, Aunt Cissy and Uncle John would stay with the MacLeays at Oakbank. John might return to his practice, but he was sure Cissy would remain longer in the country.

Curiously, a few weeks after the Melbourne Cup, Will received a letter with a Sydney postmark. A long time had passed since school days in the harbour city, so he was puzzled as to who might be writing to him. Opening the letter revealed an unexpected and delightful surprise. Mr Kent, their respected teacher, had read in the Sydney newspapers of Will's extraordinary ride on Stardust in the Melbourne Cup. He congratulated his former pupil, expressing how much joy this news had given him. Mindful of the tragedies the Scott brothers had suffered, Mr Kent shared they often were in his thoughts, and he trusted that both were well. Added to this sentence was a footnote: *'Clearly there is no question that the rider of Stardust is healthy and well!'* he wrote. *'The race sounded extraordinary!'* Should David or William ever visit Sydney, Mr Kent and his wife would be delighted to see them. Will was very touched to receive this kind letter which he looked forward to sharing with David at Christmas. Letter writing was not his strong point, but Will was so touched with Mr Kent's thoughtful note that he carefully and meticulously wrote a reply. One thing beyond question was that Mr Kent would never judge him. Often the boys laughed remembering one of their teacher's favourite quotes, which was that everyone faces difficulties in life: *'But just remember, boys, no one gets off Scott free!'*

After the excitement of the Melbourne Cup and all the country cousins staying at Elwood, Alistair chose to enjoy a few restful days. Will's ride had been amazing and how truly blessed was he with his family. Naturally there was diversity as the lineage expanded, but together they all got along well. He missed his darling Jane, but never did he regret their joint and courageous decision to flee the Highlands and settle in this new and now rapidly developing colony. Sandy and Lottie were never far from his thoughts, while Tam, Cissy and his beautiful grandchildren had brought so much joy into his life. That Jane's two brothers, Duncan and Hunter, had travelled vast distances across the world to see her was significant. He knew she would love to have visited Philadelphia, but for them such a venture was never possible.

They had supported themselves, but funds for such a journey were not a reality.

Communication with Archie and Martha back in Scotland had been constant, as with Samuel and Elizabeth Cobden. Neither couple had ever seen each other again, but letters had kept them up to date with life in the Highlands, while Alistair had assisted several families whom Reverend Cobden had directed to New South Wales. Overall, it had been a very privileged and extraordinary life. No one's time on earth was free of trials, but Alistair, as he reminisced, viewed his with much gratitude.

He held few regrets. His brother's gift of pounds to enable his elopement with Jane had been repaid through a transfer from the Bank of New South Wales to Archie's account in the Bank of Scotland. He and his dearly loved wife had endured heartbreaking losses, but their shared life had been special. One didn't have to look far to see other people's tragedies.

Although his main residence was with his daughter Cissy and John at their Elwood home, quite a lot of time was enjoyed at Oakbank with Tam's family, as well as with his grandson Will at Amaru. A train up to the Murray these days was much simpler than a horse and cart and it also enabled Alistair to interact with Jane's brother Duncan and his family at Argyll.

So many changes had occurred during his time in this colony and very soon Australia would be declared a Federation with six states and one territory. In some ways,

Alistair regretted that he had not travelled to Queensland, Tasmania, Western Australia, South Australia or the Northern Territory, but it was such a vast country. Acquaintances who had made these journeys described time there, in wonderful detail. Despite his first 20 years in Scotland, Alistair had only ever travelled to Inverness until he and Jane had trekked across the Highlands.

A week after the exciting race, Alistair chose to revisit the Murray. Christmas would be lovely but hectic, hence this interlude. Tam collected his father at the Echuca Railway Station, and drove to Oakbank. The countryside was much greener and fresher than during the Easter holiday. Alistair loved being with Cissy and John at their Elwood home, but something innate within him came alive whenever he returned to the country. A few days were spent with Tam, Grace, Robert and Rose, which he loved. Sandy's grave by the riverbank was always a place of quiet contemplation. What might his gifted son's life have been, his father so often wondered? Having loved his brief stay at Oakbank, Tam then drove his father across to Will at Amaru. Whether it was Lottie, his dearly loved, deceased daughter and Will's devoted mother, or mutual love of life on the banks of the Murray, who knew, but a special bond existed between these two. Alistair loved all his family equally, but an innate connection existed between himself and Will. As it was no longer safe for Alistair to mount a horse, Will drove him round the station in his cart, sharing all the activities presently underway. Sheep soon to be shorn, ponies being broken in and irrigation schemes being trialled. They loved this time together. After an enjoyable and relaxing week, Will drove his grandfather into the town where he caught the train back to Melbourne. In just a few weeks, he would be back again with all the family for Christmas.

On arrival in the city, Alistair hired a carriage to Elwood. Cissy welcomed her father home again with much love. Alistair shared with the Elwood household the happy time he had enjoyed on the Murray, with Tam's family and his grandson. *'Everyone,'* he said, *'was looking forward to seeing their Melbourne cousins in a few weeks!'* Farm life always revived Alistair. The school holidays and Christmas were fast approaching. During their delicious dinner, respective stories were shared. Oakbank was very productive, with Robert working full time with his father, whilst Will was doing exceptionally well with his horse stud and a sizeable flock of sheep. Familiar with life on the river homesteads, they all related to Grandy's news.

After dinner they went to the sitting room, where Sylvie played some excellent piano recitals. Very impressed, everyone applauded her enthusiastically. Cissy then replaced her niece at the piano and commenced playing her father's favourite Scottish classic, 'The Bonnie Banks of Loch Lomond'. Everyone listened passionately until towards the end Alistair commenced singing, followed by all the family. Their enthusiasm and passion for this much-loved

Scottish classic ensured that it was played a second time with everyone joining in. Cissy's last recital for the evening was Beethoven's 'Moonlight Sonata'. This beautiful music permeated the room, leaving everyone with an exquisite sense of serenity. Feeling at peace with the world, but weary after the past fortnight, Alistair wished everyone goodnight and headed off to bed.

In the morning, believing him to be in need of extra rest, Cissy refrained from disturbing her father, until eventually she delivered his morning cup of tea. During the night, Alistair had died. In shock, Cissy hastily summoned John from his practice. After a brief examination, her loving husband held her in his arms, whispering in her ear that her father's passing was *'a reward for a good life'*. He had been taken peacefully in his sleep. *'If only we could all depart that way,'* he added.

As they quietly rested together on the couch, reminiscing about Alistair and Jane's life and the wonderful legacy they had entrusted to their children, it certainly was apparent that the intrepid Scottish elopers, overall, had enjoyed blessed and fortunate lives. John also communicated that the generous and caring way his wife and her brother Tam had cared for their father, especially since Jane's death, would always be a source of comfort to them. Absorbing these loving words, Cissy was prompted to look back over her own life and its challenges. While having no children of their own had been a heartbreak, how blessed were she and John to care for, love and influence her sister Lottie's three special offspring.

Arrangements were made for Alistair to be laid to rest beside his dearly loved wife, and ample time was allowed so that all their family and friends could be together on this sad but memorable occasion. The MacLeays and Sinclairs had not long returned from the Melbourne Cup, but of course everyone came to Elwood for Grandy's funeral. There was profound sadness, but also gratitude for his life and that of his darling Jane. Alistair's family would miss him so much, but they all appreciated that it had been a life well lived and he had been blessed with a swift and painless exit. Alistair and Jane had profoundly influenced their children and grandchildren's lives, ensuring their legacy most certainly would live on.

Characters

Jane Sinclair	Alistair MacLeay *Husband*	
James Sinclair	*Father*	
Walter Sinclair	*Brother*	
Hunter Sinclair	*Brother*	Jeanie *Wife*
Hector, Jane, Douglas, Jock	*Children*	
Gordon Sinclair	*Brother*	
Duncan Sinclair	*Brother*	Jess *Wife*
Campbell, Maisie, Stuart	*Children*	
Alistair MacLeay	*Husband of Jane Sinclair*	
Sandy MacLeay	*Son*	
Lottie MacLeay	*Daughter*	Angus Scott *Husband*
David, William, Sylvie	*Children*	
Tam MacLeay	*Son*	Grace Smith *Wife*
Richard, Robert, Rose	*Children*	
Cissy MacLeay	*Daughter*	John Wallace *Husband*
Archie MacLeay	*Brother of Alistair MacLeay*	
Martha MacLeay	*Wife of Archie*